MATE FOR T~~HREE~~

Pack Law 3

Becca Van

MENAGE EVERLASTING

Siren Publishing, Inc.
www.SirenPublishing.com

A SIREN PUBLISHING BOOK
IMPRINT: Ménage Everlasting

MATE FOR THREE
Copyright © 2012 by Becca Van

ISBN: 978-1-62241-120-7

First Printing: June 2012

Cover design by Les Byerley
All art and logo copyright © 2012 by Siren Publishing, Inc.

Printed in the U.S.A.

PUBLISHER
Siren Publishing, Inc.
www.SirenPublishing.com

DEDICATION

To the best sister in the world. You keep me sane. Love you, Deb.

MATE FOR THREE

Pack Law 3

BECCA VAN
Copyright © 2012

Chapter One

Talia Black didn't have time for this shit. She heard a pop, and then the steering wheel became heavy and her car became hard to steer. She lifted her foot from the accelerator and pulled onto the side of the road. The last thing she needed was to have to change a tire in the dead of night on a strange road. She kept her headlights on and pushed the button for her hazards, then got out of her car.

She opened the trunk and rummaged around for the jack. The light in the trunk was so small and dim she could barely make out the apparatus. She pulled it from the trunk and lifted the baseboard that hid the spare wheel. There was nothing there. Fucking hell, she'd forgotten she had needed a new spare and had taken the old one out to be repaired, but the garage had called and told her the old tire was irreparable and would need to be replaced. She hadn't remembered to pick up a new one.

Talia shivered when she heard rustling in the undergrowth off to the side of the road, mere feet from where she stood. She turned her head and saw the glowing eyes of an animal staring at her. Her heart rate picked up, and her breathing escalated with panic. She had no idea what animal it was and felt sweat break out on her skin. She stared intently, and she could just make out the silhouette of a large dog. Not wanting to alarm the animal, she closed the trunk lid with a quiet snick. She wanted to get away and back into the safety of her car, but she didn't want to move too quickly. She inched her way toward the driver's side door and slid in behind the wheel, closing and locking the door behind her.

She kept her eyes on whatever animal was staring at her and jumped as a large black wolf strode out of the bushes. It moved up close to her car and sniffed the air. She watched as it threw its massive head up and howled. The mournful sound sent shivers racing up and down her spine, causing goose bumps to erupt all over her skin. The animal was huge, and she shuddered with awe as she watched it howl to the moon. She wondered if it was communicating with its pack or if it was just singing with joy.

The wolf lowered and tilted its head. It looked as if it were studying her just as intently as she was studying it. It walked around to the front of her car, keeping its eyes on her the whole time. The animal was huge. Its massive shoulders were taller than the hood of her car. Its head was slightly taller than hers as she sat there staring into its golden, glowing eyes. She saw its black coat as it passed the glare of her shining headlights. It didn't take its eyes off her. It opened its huge mouth, and she caught sight of the wolf's shining white teeth as its tongue lolled out to the side. It looked like it was grinning at her. She felt like prey to a predator, and her thoughts briefly flashed back to Paul. She shook her head and shoved her paranoia to the back of her mind. It walked up to the driver's side door, sniffed, let out another howl, and then it disappeared into the trees and bushes on the other side of the road.

"Wow. That was just a little too close to nature," Talia muttered to herself. But she pushed those thoughts aside. The wolf had been alarming, but something much more frightening was out there.

What the hell was she going to do now? She rummaged in her purse, looking for her cell phone. She was going to have to call for a tow truck. Not that she had the money to spare for such things, but what else could she do? She needed to keep moving. She couldn't afford to spend hours on the side of the road. He would be looking for her, and no matter what she did, no matter where she went, he always seemed to find her. She had tried to leave once before, and he had tracked her down and dragged her back. She wondered if she would ever be totally free of him.

She turned her headlights off as she gripped her phone. If she called for a tow truck, her name would end up on a computer somewhere and he would find her. She dropped her cell into her lap and covered her face, giving in to tears for the first time since she had escaped his clutches six weeks ago.

Once the storm was over, she reached for the box of tissues in her center console, wiped her tears away, and blew her nose. She had no idea what to do, and she was totally stranded.

Talia glanced in her rearview mirror when she saw a flash of light. Headlights were coming up behind her. She slid down in her seat and hoped she was hidden from view. She reached into her purse for the can of Mace and clutched it tightly. The lights were bright, and she held her breath as she waited for the car to pass. Only it didn't pass.

She saw the large vehicle pull up behind her in the side mirror, and she began to panic. *God, how did he find me so soon? Please, protect me from the monster.* She saw the shadow of a large male walking toward her and pulled the Mace out of her purse. She clutched the can so tightly her knuckles were aching.

She jumped and screamed when the man tapped on her closed window. She looked up and thought she saw his eyes glowing in the light from the car behind. She was too scared to open her window and had no intention of doing so. This might not be who she was afraid it was. She was so afraid, alone, and vulnerable, and she was sick to death of being frightened.

"Are you all right, ma'am? Do you need some help?"

The sound of his deep voice sent shivers running along her spine, but not with fear this time. She felt it wrap around her, and her pussy clenched and dripped fluid onto her panties.

"Um, is there a tow truck close by?" Talia asked through her closed window.

"There is a truck in Aztec, about twenty miles back. I see you have a flat tire. I can change it for you if you like."

Talia looked up at him as he turned toward the glow of his own car's headlights. Her breath hitched as she got her first good sight of the giant man. He had short, dark hair, wide, muscular shoulders, and biceps which strained at the cotton of his white T-shirt. His chest tapered down to a flat belly, slim hips, and massive, strong thighs. She couldn't see the color of his eyes, but as her gaze wandered up to his face, her eyes caught on the hint of dimples on either side of his mouth. He had a full lower lip, and the upper one was thinner. She saw his lips quirk up at the ends and knew she had been caught staring at him.

Talia lowered her eyes but slid them sideways when she realized her eyes were on his crotch. She felt her cheeks heat with embarrassment and hoped to goodness he hadn't seen her checking out what looked to be an impressive package. She knew he had asked her something, but she couldn't for the life of her remember what it had been. *Come on, Talia. Get your mind out of the gutter.*

"Ma'am, do you want me to change your tire?"

"Uh, that would be great, but you can't. I don't have a spare," Talia stated.

"Well, that would certainly prevent me from changing your tire. I live five minutes down the road. A lot of my cousins and friends are there, too, so you wouldn't be alone with me. You're welcome to stay the night if you want to. Until you can get a new spare. My name is Dr. Blayk Friess. I don't like leaving you here all alone. It's not safe. Why don't you grab your stuff and I'll take you back to my house and you can stay in the guest bedroom?"

"Do you have any ID?" Talia asked cautiously.

"Sure," Blayk answered.

Talia watched warily as Blayk reached into the back pocket of his jeans and withdrew his wallet. He flipped it open and held it toward her, but with the light from his car shining onto the plastic, she couldn't see properly.

"Can you take it out?" Talia asked then lowered her window a crack. Blayk pulled his license from his wallet and slid it through the small gap and handed it to her.

Talia turned on her interior light and studied the small plastic card. He was definitely who he said he was, and he hadn't tried to force his way into her car or tried to coax her out. She turned the light off, unlocked the door, and got out.

She was glad when he moved back away from her a few feet with his hands nonthreatening in the pockets of his jeans. The man was so tall that she still had to crick her neck back to see his face, and he was at least two arm's lengths away from her. Talia knew she was rather under average in height, but Dr. Blayk Friess was a giant. The top of her head didn't quite reach the middle of his chest. He had to be at least six foot four. Her hand brushed his as she handed the tall man back his license. She sucked in a breath as a warm tingle ran from her hand, up her arm, over her breasts, and down to her now-aching pussy.

"Thank you," Talia said quietly.

"You're welcome. Now, have you decided what you would like to do?" he asked her.

"Well, I really don't have much of a choice. I would be very grateful if I could spend the night in your spare room."

"Okay," Blayk said. "Is there anything you will need for the night, ma'am?"

Talia indicated one of her bags in the backseat of her car with her hand and then realized she hadn't told the man her name.

"Oh, I'm so sorry. I'm Talia Black," Talia said, extending her hand to Blayk.

Talia was surprised when, instead of taking her hand and shaking it, he took her hand in his, bent over, and kissed the back of it.

"I am very delighted to meet you, Talia," Blayk said. "Now, which bags would you like to take?"

"Oh, just the small one on the backseat, thank you," Talia said and watched as Blayk skirted around her, opened the door, and reached in to retrieve her bag. She locked the doors and followed Blayk back to his truck.

Talia was glad she wouldn't have to spend the night afraid and alone in her car. She knew she wouldn't have gotten much sleep. She was still too nervous to relax, knowing somehow, someway, he would always find her.

She felt an immediate affinity with Dr. Blayk Friess. She couldn't explain why she felt that way. She just did. Having other people around her would lessen her anxiety, and maybe even enable her to sleep the night through, which would be a blessing.

She was so tired. Her body felt heavy with fatigue, her eyes sore and tired. She felt as if her eyeballs were about to pop out of their sockets. Maybe by staying with this man and his family, her ex, Paul, would lose the trail. She sighed as she realized that was a near impossibility. He would be able to follow her scent trail as easily as a hound dog.

Blayk held the passenger door open for her, and she gaped at the large vehicle. She supposed, since he was so big, he would obviously need a big truck, but she was going to have a struggle getting up into the beast. The dilemma was solved for her when Blayk placed his hands around her waist, picked her up with ease, and placed her gently on the seat.

She stared up at him and saw he was looking at her with hunger. She wondered if she should get out of the truck and run like hell, because she felt reciprocal hunger firing up inside her and it scared the crap out of her. She couldn't afford to feel anything for anyone right now. She didn't need this. She would spend the night in his guest bedroom, and in the morning she would get a new tire and a spare for the trunk and leave.

She sat quietly in awe as Blayk drove up the gravel drive five minutes later. The sight of the large, colonial-style mansion made her speechless. She'd never seen anything so beautiful in her life. She took a deep breath as Blayk pulled the truck into a large carport. She opened her door and slid to the ground before he had a chance to help her. The last thing she wanted right now was to have his hands back on her, causing her body to go up in flames again. She met Blayk at the front of the vehicle and hesitated when he began to lead the way to a door. *What the hell am I doing? I don't know this man. I should have stayed in my car.*

Talia let her breath out slowly when Blayk stopped and turned toward her. She watched as he walked the few paces between them until he was standing at her side.

"You have nothing to be afraid of, baby. I won't hurt you and neither will any of the people inside. Come on, let's get you settled. You look like you could use a good night's sleep," Blayk stated.

You have no idea. Blayk held his hand out toward her. Talia looked and ran possible scenarios through her mind, but she really didn't have much of a choice. Well, she did, but she was curious as to why the man before her drew her. She took his hand and felt as if her life had just changed irrevocably.

Chapter Two

Talia followed Blayk through the door and gasped at the sight of the beautiful interior. She couldn't believe the luxury of the place, and she was still only in the hallway. There was money practically dripping from the walls. Talia began to feel uncomfortable. She was a lowly receptionist at a hotel for goodness' sake. She didn't belong here.

"Come on, baby. I'll show you around," Blayk stated, pulling her from her trance.

Talia followed and stayed slightly behind him when he led her into a massive living room. There were people everywhere. She wondered if they all lived here or if they were just guests. He pulled her over to where three large, handsome men sat with a small woman.

"Everyone, this is Talia Black. Talia, these are my cousins Jonah, Mikhail, and Brock Friess and their m—wife, Michelle," Blayk stated.

What? Three husbands? "Nice to meet you all," Talia replied, hoping her shock didn't show on her face.

"On behalf of everyone here, welcome, Talia," Jonah said.

"Come on, I'll show you to your room. You can meet everyone else later," Blayk said.

Talia followed Blayk and couldn't help looking back into the room as she left. She saw a few of the men sniffing the air and wondered if she needed a shower. *What's up with that?* She felt the hair on her nape stand on end. Something about their behavior struck her as familiar, but she couldn't put her finger on why that was.

Blayk led her up a wide staircase then up another set of steps. He led her to the left of the long hall on the third story of the house. She followed along, but she felt as if she were moving on automatic. Something wasn't right here, but she couldn't put her finger on the pulse, so to speak. She was too exhausted to ask or even wonder further. Blayk stopped at the end of the hall and opened the door. He pulled her into a normal-size sitting room, and she sighed with relief. At least something in the house seemed normal. He led her farther into the room and across to a doorway on the other side. He showed her the bathroom and then to a small guest bedroom with a queen-size bed.

"This is the spare room in the suite I share with my two brothers, Chris and James. We each have our own room. I hope you will be comfortable here, Talia," Blayk said as he turned to look at her.

"Thank you. I know I will. Thanks for all your help, Blayk. I'll be out of your hair tomorrow morning, as soon as I can arrange for a new tire and of course a spare," Talia said as she nervously gripped her purse.

"There's no rush, baby. Stay as long as you need to. Okay?"

"Thanks."

Talia heard a door slam and jumped at the loud noise. She turned toward the door and froze, and her breath stalled in her throat as she saw two men looking in at her. She backed up a step and flinched as she bumped into Blayk's hard, warm body. She sidestepped the large man until she was against the far wall, her amazement at the sight of the two handsome men making it difficult for her to breathe.

"Talia, I'd like you to meet my brothers, Chris and James. Guys, this is Talia Black," Blayk stated.

"Hey, sugar, pleased to meet you," James said and stepped forward, offering her a hand.

"You, too," Talia replied as she took his hand. She felt her eyes widen as she shook hands with James. The same tingling warmth and sexual arousal traveled through her as it had done when her skin had brushed Blayk's. When he released her, Chris offered his hand, and she had the same reaction. *What the fuck?*

"Nice to meet you, Talia," Chris said in a voice so deep she shivered.

"You, too," Talia replied, words nearly beyond her comprehension. She was so entranced by the three men that she was having difficulty getting her mind and body to cooperate. Talia had thought Blayk was tall, and he was, but Chris was even taller.

Chris had to be in the vicinity of six feet six inches. He had light, sandy-brown hair and brown eyes with gold flecks. He had sharp cheekbones, and his square jaw was classically handsome. He was the most muscular of the three brothers, but his physique was not quite the bodybuilder type. He was solid and big.

She slid her eyes over to James. He was the shortest of the three at around six foot two, with light-blue eyes and blond hair. He was pure, solid muscle, with wide, broad shoulders and bulging biceps, and handsome in a harsh, rugged way. He had light-blond stubble on his jaw and an indent in his square chin. She moved her gaze over to Blayk again. He had a dark-olive complexion with his black hair and blue eyes. He wasn't as muscular as James or Chris, but he was still well toned.

"Are you all right, baby?" Blayk asked.

"Yes," Talia replied and cringed mentally at the sound of her high-pitched voice.

"Are you hungry, sugar?" James asked.

"No, thank you."

"Why don't we leave you to it? Make yourself at home, darlin', use anything you like," Chris stated. "We'll be in the living room."

Talia watched warily as the three men left her to get settled. She relaxed for the first time since Blayk had found her sitting in her car on the lonely, quiet, dark road. She grabbed some clean clothes from her bag, opened the door to the bedroom, and peeked out. She sighed with relief when she saw no one and headed to the bathroom. At least she'd be able to shower tonight. Who knew when she would be able to get clean again? She intended to be out of here as soon as she could arrange it.

* * * *

"What's she so scared of, bro?" Chris asked.

Blayk looked up at Chris as he sat down across from him. "I have no idea. She's hardly spoken a word to me beyond introducing herself."

"Where did you meet her?" James asked.

"I was on a run and I smelled her. I found her on the road no more than five minutes north of here. She was sitting in her car. She had a flat and I offered to change her tire for her but she had no spare."

"Shit, that's not good. Where is she from?" Chris asked.

"I don't know. As I said we haven't gotten beyond the introductions. I'll need your help to get her to open up. She had a couple of boxes in her car and a suitcase. She's either moving or she's on the run," Blayk stated.

"What do you think?" Chris asked. "What's your gut telling you?"

"She's in trouble and she's on the run," Blayk replied.

"I agree. She's so skittish. When we walked into the room I could smell her fear. She was nearly panicking. Her heartbeat was fast and so was her breathing," James stated.

"How the fuck are we going to get her to trust us and stay here? We can't let her leave. She's our mate," Chris said.

"She obviously trusts you, Blayk, otherwise she wouldn't be here. How did you get her to come home with you?" James asked.

"I offered her the spare room and I showed her my ID. I think the fact that I'm a doctor helped to sway her decision. Plus I don't think she has anywhere else to go, and by the looks of the heap of junk she's driving, she has no money either."

"She's such a tiny little thing. She can't be much over five foot. Man, the top of her head doesn't even reach up to my chest. She is so petite, I'd be scared of hurting her when I touch her," Chris said with a sigh.

"Boy, does she have curves in all the right places. And her hair. God I've never seen such white, fine hair before. Her eyes are gorgeous, they remind me of the deep blue sea," Chris said with a groan.

"My wolf's pushing against me already to claim her. What the hell are we going to do? She says she'll be out of our hair first thing in the morning. How the hell do we keep our mate here and then break the news to her that we are werewolves? She is going to freak out. She's already scared shitless. I don't want to frighten her any more than she already is," Blayk said with a sigh.

"I think we just have to take one step at a time. If she leaves we have to follow. We can't keep her here against her will. So we follow her and woo her. Blayk, you set it up with Jonah to get someone ready to take over our duties if need be. Did you get her license plate number?" Chris asked.

"Yeah," Blayk replied and told his older brother the number. "Are you going to run it?"

"What do you think?"

Chris walked over to the dining table where his laptop was on and open and Blayk followed. He watched as his brother ran Talia's car plate. Talia was from Twin Falls, Idaho. He watched as Chris pulled up a search for "Talia Black from Idaho" on the Idaho statewide repository. Blayk was glad they had access to this information since he managed security for the Friess Pack along with his brothers. What came up on the screen blew him away.

Talia had been married for a year but was now divorced. Her ex-husband, Paul Rogan, had used Talia as a punching bag. He felt his fury rise and his blood boil as Chris clicked on picture after picture. His wolf pushed against him, wanting to change and go find the bastard who had hurt his mate. The sight of their small woman so bruised and battered made him sick to his stomach. Her eyes had been swollen shut, her jaw and face bruised beyond recognition. The fact that the motherfucker who had hit her had gotten off on good behavior nearly made his wolf howl. He wanted to hunt down that bastard and rip him apart. His brother looked up at him, and he saw the same fury on Chris's face. James moved toward him and looked over Chris's shoulder at the laptop monitor.

"Motherfucker," James roared.

Blayk could see James was having as much trouble controlling his beast as he had. His brother's eyes were a glowing gold color. A sound and the clean scent of his mate drifted to him on the air. He looked up to see Talia standing uncertainly in the doorway to the living room. She looked like a scared rabbit.

He longed to go to her and take her into his arms. He wanted to mark her and know she would be under his and his brothers' protection. He wanted to know everything about her, but most of all he wanted to be able to love her. But not just in the physical sense. Of course he wanted to claim her and make love to her, but he wanted to show her he loved her already. That love was part of her being his mate. He wanted to shower her with love, respect, and affection, but he knew he would scare her off if he did. So he took a deep breath, trying to get his rage back under control, and walked over to her. He stopped in front of her and slowly reached for her hand.

"Are you okay, baby?" Blayk asked.

"Yes, thanks. But my name is not sugar, baby, or darlin'," Talia stated as she looked up at him. "My name is Talia, use it."

"Sure thing, baby," Blayk replied and was pleased to see her eyes shooting daggers at him. That meant that ex-bastard of hers had not beaten the spirit out of her. He led her to the sofa and sat down beside her. James rushed over and sat on her other side. She looked from him to James, and he could see the cogs in her mind turning as she frowned at him and his brother.

"Did you say your cousins shared a wife?" Talia asked.

"Yes, they are all brothers and they fell in love with the same woman. They were lucky enough that she fell in love with them, and she accepted them all as her husbands," Blayk explained.

"But that isn't even legal. How the hell could she marry three men at once? How she can even deal with that many men is a mystery. Dealing with one, let alone three, is a complete nightmare," Talia stated.

Blayk didn't think Talia had meant to say those words out loud. He watched her cheeks turn red, and she lowered her eyes. She looked so afraid sitting there between him and James, but so damn right. He leaned toward her, intoxicated by her scent, and sniffed the fragrant skin of her neck. He looked down into her eyes when she turned toward him. He could see her fear and uncertainty, but he could also see and smell her desire. He held her eyes with his and lowered his head slowly. He heard her heart rate speed up as well as her breathing. Her eyes widened with surprise, her pupils dilated, and her eyes changed from a deep blue to almost violet. He kept his eyes connected with hers, as he slowly brushed his lips against her soft, moist flesh.

He didn't force or demand, and he didn't open his mouth. He just tantalized her, sliding his lips back and forth in a light caress. He felt her sweet breath sigh against his mouth as she exhaled. He kept his hands to himself and only touched her with his lips. He was about to pull back and give her room, but his little mate surprised the hell out of him.

Talia reached up and wrapped her arms around his neck, closed her eyes, and opened her mouth under his. She became the aggressor in the mating of their mouths. She slid her tongue over his lips, and he was lost. He opened his mouth and took back control of the kiss. He wrapped his tongue around hers, pulling it into his mouth, and he sucked on her. He groaned as he clasped her around the waist, pulling her onto his lap. She was so small and light he barely felt her weight. But, man, did she have curves. He felt her breasts crush against him as she opened herself up to him and he devoured her. She tasted so sweet. He was nearly drunk on her flavor.

He felt his wolf pushing at him to claim her and knew he had to pull back so he could get a hold of his control. He slowed the kiss until he was sipping at her lips and then eased back away from her.

He could smell the musk of her dripping cunt and felt his wolf butt up and push him, demanding to be let loose. He saw Talia's eyes widen, and then she was trying to get free. He let her go instantly, aware she needed space and time to get herself back under control. What he didn't expect to see was suspicion in her eyes.

"What are you?" Talia asked in a whisper and rose to her feet.

"Talia, don't be scared of us. We would never hurt you. In fact we would give our lives to keep you safe," Blayk stated.

Blayk watched as she continued to back away and was glad when Chris moved up behind her to stop her falling over the coffee table and hurting herself. She bumped into Chris, and she tilted her head up and back. She surprised him again when she didn't pull away from his brother this time. She just stood there staring up at Chris, and he could smell the feminine scent of her creaming cunt. He watched and waited to see what she would do.

"She needs to know. Since she's asked I am going to tell her what we are and where she fits in. The sooner she knows everything the sooner we can start courting her," Chris said to him and James using their telepathic link.

"Talia, just remember we would never hurt you, okay?" Blayk pleaded.

"Okay," Talia replied.

Blayk watched her carefully and smiled when he realized she was leaning against Chris. She probably wasn't even aware of how telling her trust was in that moment, but he was, and he knew his brothers were, too. Chris reached down and picked Talia up into his arms. He had an arm beneath her knees and another around her shoulders. Blayk's brother carried their mate to a large armchair across from him and James. Talia didn't seem to be worried to find herself on a strange man's lap, which he was thankful for. His brother still had one of his arms wrapped around Talia's waist, holding her still while she looked at him expectantly.

"We are werewolves, Talia. And you are our mate," Blayk explained and watched her intently. She surprised him yet again. She snuggled up against Chris, resting her head against Chris's torso, smiled, and closed her eyes.

"Oh shit. Out of the frying pan into the fire," Talia whispered shakily, and her body went rigid with tension.

"I don't want you getting mad with us, darlin', but we ran your license plates to find out about you and then we checked your name through the police database. We know about your ex, Talia. We know what he did to you. Are you on the run from him? Does he know where you are?" Chris asked.

Talia had sat up when Chris had begun to speak. At first she looked outraged and then resigned. She glared at him, James, and Chris. She pushed away from Chris and rose to her feet. She paced the away and then back again.

"You could have just asked me. Why did you do that? Why did you go behind my back like that? He's going to come for me. You see, my ex is also a werewolf. He is the Beta of a small pack in Idaho. I met him just as I was finishing college. It was a whirlwind romance. We were married within a month. His Alpha is his brother. He didn't even bat an eye when Paul beat me for some infraction in front of the whole pack. In fact his brother encouraged it. Paul knew I wasn't his mate, but he married me anyway. He took great delight in telling me that the last time he beat me. He told me I was just a piece of ass to keep himself occupied with until his real mate came along. I organized a restraining order against him while I was recovering in hospital and filed for divorce.

"My divorce came through four weeks ago, just as I was being released from the hospital, and I left. I have been on the road ever since. I know all about werewolves and how they treat their mates. I know you think I am your mate. Maybe I am and maybe I'm not, but there is no way in hell I am letting you claim me or tell me what to do," Talia stated.

Blayk was in shock. No wonder she hadn't batted an eye when he had told her what they were. But the situation she had been in had just made their lives a hell of a lot harder. He had no idea how they were going to get Talia to accept him and his brothers as her mates, much less how to heal the pain he heard behind her words.

Chapter Three

"Talia, what you have been through, I can only imagine. But please believe me when I say we would never ever hurt you. We won't claim you without your consent and we will protect you from any danger. I don't know what the pack you lived with taught you, but we don't work that way. We cherish our mates. If you don't believe me just go and ask our Alphas' mate, Michelle, or our cousins' mate, Keira," Chris stated.

"Look, I know you believe that, and maybe it's even true. But to date, my experience has proved to me that men can't be trusted. Actions always speak louder than words. I'm not going to lie to you. I am attracted to all of you, but I am not willing to act on that chemistry. I've been there, done that before. Do you really think I am going to jump from one fire to another without questioning?" Talia asked.

"Baby, I…we understand you have reservations, but we promise we won't ever hurt you. Please, stay here with us where we can keep you safe. We won't pressure you at all. You have never lived with your true mates before. Please give us a chance to show you we are nothing like your ex," Blayk pleaded.

Chris watched Talia as she nibbled on her lower lip. His cock had been hard since the moment he had smelled her scent in the house. His balls were aching, and he wanted to pick her up, strip her naked, and bury himself balls-deep in her hot, wet cunt. But he knew that wasn't an option.

He was the eldest out of the three of them at the age of thirty-four. He and his brothers had been hoping to meet their mate for over ten years, but since their Alphas and their other cousins had found their own women, that yearning had tripled. It had been wonderful to watch all his cousins interact with their mates and woo them into their lives and their beds. But it had also been hard. He hadn't felt envious of any of his family members until recently. Now that he and his brothers had their mate in their den, the knot of jealousy had diminished. He knew it wasn't going to be easy to convince Talia they were worth the risk to love and mate with, but there was no way in hell he was giving up.

"Okay. You have a deal. I will stay here, for now. But if you guys put one foot wrong or try to lay a hand on me without my permission, I will cut your balls off and shove them down your throat," Talia stated resolutely.

"You won't need to do that, darlin'. You get to make the first move," Chris said with determination.

"Do you promise?" Talia asked, tears in her eyes as she looked at him.

"Yes, darlin', I promise," Chris replied.

Chris saw Talia's shoulders sag as the tension in her muscles released for the first time. She looked so damn tired and lonely. He wanted to wrap her up and never let her go. She surprised him by moving toward him and giving him a hug.

"Thank you," Talia whispered.

Chris watched as she straightened and turned to his brothers.

"Do you two promise as well?" Talia asked.

Chris had to bite his tongue as she stood with her hands on her hips and glared at Blayk and James. She was so full of passion and fire. He couldn't wait to tap into that appetite and set her free. He knew her ex had never touched her heart or her desire. He couldn't explain how he knew, but he just did.

"I promise, baby," Blayk replied.

"I promise, sugar," James stated.

"Okay then. I'm glad that's settled," Talia said.

She turned toward Chris and surprised him yet again. Talia climbed onto his lap and snuggled against him. She reminded him of a kitten with her spitting and claws, but when she was happy, she was content to curl up and cuddle. Chris wrapped an arm around her waist and pulled her in close to him. Her scent permeated his senses, and he inhaled deeply. His wolf had settled down and was waiting, ready to claim his mate, but willing to be patient for the moment. He only hoped his beast wouldn't push too hard or become too impatient and take over. The shit would definitely hit the fan if he or his brothers claimed Talia before she was ready.

He was going to have to run every night and jack off, too, just to keep control over his animal. It would be worth it though. The thought of finally having her come to him and his brothers so they could claim her was a dream he'd had for many years. He wasn't willing to shelve that dream now that they had finally found her.

Chris looked down when her heard Talia's breathing change. She was sound asleep. She looked like an angel, with her long white-blonde hair flowing around her face and over her shoulders. Her light eyelashes were barely visible against her creamy skin. He knew then that no matter what she said, she already trusted them. If she didn't she wouldn't have let Blayk bring her home, and she wouldn't be curled up on his lap. He studied the dark smudges beneath her eyes and felt his anger begin to boil again. The thought of her ex laying into her in front of his Alpha brother and no one helping her was too hard for him to comprehend. How anyone could treat any woman like that was just so alien to him, but the fact that she was his mate and had been seriously injured made his gut churn.

She was so tiny compared to him and his brothers, but he knew beneath the fragile exterior she had a core of steel. She wouldn't have survived if she didn't. He knew she was going to fit into the pack really easily. He wouldn't have been surprised if she ended up being best friends with Michelle and Keira. He could just see the three of them keeping him, his brothers, and his cousins running around in circles after them. He smiled and closed his eyes, savoring the feel of his sleeping mate in his arms.

"She's gorgeous, isn't she," Blayk said, using their mental link.

"Fuck yeah. I'm nearly too scared to touch her," James stated.

"She might look fragile, but she is so strong inside. You saw the way she negotiated with us. Where those the actions of a delicate little rose?" Chris asked his brothers.

"No. She is strong and feisty and so fucking gorgeous. My cock is so hard I could pound nails," Blayk stated.

"Yeah, I'm in the same boat, bro. Her scent just wraps around you and won't let go. My wolf has been pacing since I caught her scent in the house," James stated.

"Mine, too. Make sure you run in your wolf form every night and jack off if the desire gets too intense. We can't let our beasts take control and claim her. We can't betray her trust that way. She would run, and we'd never see her again," Chris explained.

"Yeah, we know, Chris. In fact I think I'll go for a run now," Blayk said.

"I'm with you, man. Then I'm hitting the shower," James said.

Chris closed his eyes as his brothers left their rooms. He was content to just sit where he was holding his woman curled up in his lap. He leaned his head back and listened to the beat of his heart. He was content and felt complete for the first time in a very long while, and he hadn't even claimed her yet.

How long Chris just sat there holding Talia he had no idea. The time passed swiftly, and he could hear pack members coming and going. He decided he and his brothers were going to have to look into her ex and the pack he belonged to. He wanted to question Talia further about the pack she had been mixed up in, but he would wait until tomorrow. He didn't want to disturb her from what was obviously much-needed rest. She had been on the road for a month, and she had only just gotten out of hospital when she'd left Idaho. No wonder she was so tired. God knew when she'd had her last decent meal.

He wanted to know everything about her. What her favorite color was, her favorite food, and where her family was. He wanted to know what her dreams had been as a child and what kind of future she dreamed of now. He craved that knowledge and could hardly wait to learn about her. But most of all he wanted to be able to love her. She had already entwined herself around his heart, and the thought of her leaving or getting hurt sent pain shooting into his chest. She was his mate, and there was no way in hell he or his brothers were going to screw this up. He planned to woo his way into her bed and her heart as soon as possible. Once he and his brothers claimed her, she was never leaving their sight. In fact she would be with one of them at all times. She needed protection, and if at all possible one of them would be with her around the clock.

Chris opened his eyes when she stirred in his arms and whimpered. Her breathing was fast and loud, and her eyelids twitched from the rapid movement of her eyeballs. She was dreaming, and from the look of the frown on her face and the small noises she was making, it wasn't a pleasant dream. She flinched and cried out loudly. Her arms moved up, and it looked like she was trying to protect her face. He gently took hold of her arms and pulled them down. He didn't want her hurting herself. She moved swiftly, catching him off guard, her feet kicking out, and he was thankful he wasn't on the receiving end of that kick. He caught her around the waist as she sat up and screamed. The tortured sound was so full of pain that it tore at his heart and soul. He wrapped his other arm around the front of her chest, holding her flailing arms down so she couldn't hurt herself, and began to speak to her.

"Talia, wake up. Come on, darlin', you're safe here. Wake up, Talia!"

Chris sighed with relief as she finally opened her eyes. She was still breathing heavily, but she was alert. His fury began to escalate again at the sight of terror and remembered pain in her eyes. Tears trailed down her cheeks and sparkled on her eyelashes. She looked up at him, and then she flung herself down, burying her face in his chest, and she sobbed her heart out. He held her and rocked her until the raging storm of emotions finally slowed and ceased.

"Do you want to talk about it, baby?" Chris asked gently, stroking a palm up and down her slim back.

"No."

"Do you have nightmares often?"

"All the time," Talia replied.

"Ah, baby. You're safe here, I promise. No one can get to you. We will guard you with our lives," Chris stated.

"But that's just it," Talia said as she pushed up straight again, looking into his eyes. "I don't want anyone here getting hurt because of me. I think I should just go."

"Talia, we have the best security money can buy. There are cameras and alarms with sensors all over this land and the house. No one can get in or out without somebody knowing about it. The monitors are manned all the time, and we are werewolves. You can't be anywhere safer, baby. I'm not going to make you stay if you don't want to. But just remember you are our mate, and if you leave so do we. We have been waiting to meet you for so long. We just can't let you go without following you and fighting for you. Do you understand? We can't give you up."

"I don't know what to think anymore. I am so tired and confused. I am as attracted to you and your brothers as you are to me, but I just—I need time," Talia explained.

"We all understand that, baby, and we won't force you, but you have to remember we are part animal. Our wolves are pushing at us to claim you. At the moment we are in control of our beasts, but our animal instincts are to bite you and make you ours. We don't want to hold off our wolves forever. You need to think about what you want, and when you decide, let us know," Chris said. "Now, I think it's time you were in bed. You are totally exhausted."

"Thanks, Chris. No one has ever held me and taken care of me the way you and your brothers have."

"That's only a taste of how we would look after you, baby. Imagine how much better it would be if we were mated," Chris said as he helped Talia to her feet.

He led her over to the door and saw her to her room. She gave him a wistful smile and closed the door. He didn't know how the hell he was going to survive the night, let alone days or weeks, waiting until she made her decision. But he hadn't been joking. If Talia decided to leave, then he and his brothers would definitely follow.

Chapter Four

Talia lay in bed on her side, staring at the far wall. She was too scared to fall asleep. She knew the nightmare would come again, and she didn't want her screaming to wake up the men sleeping in the other rooms. She turned over and stared through the dark, her eyes not really seeing the ceiling as she thought over what Chris and his brothers had told her. She knew the three men weren't anything like her ex-husband and his pack. Until she lay down in the guest room's big, lonely bed, she didn't realize her actions had been so telling. She had instinctively trusted Chris, Blayk, and James Friess. Otherwise she wouldn't have been in their home. She couldn't believe how she had crawled onto Chris's lap and fallen asleep. She had heard them all head to their own room's hours earlier and knew it must be well into the early hours of the morning.

Talia sighed and threw the covers back. She was thirsty and needed a drink of water. She had seen the small kitchen through the open door on the other side of the living room. So she padded out of her room, making sure she didn't make any noise, and headed to the kitchen. She flicked the light switch and searched for a glass. She had just finished drinking the water when Chris's deep voice called her name from behind her. She squealed and jumped as she spun around, the now-empty glass clutched to her chest.

"Are you okay, darlin?" Chris asked.

"Shit, you scared ten years off my life," Talia replied, looking at Chris as she sagged against the sink.

"I'm sorry. I didn't mean to scare you. Can't you sleep?"

"No," Talia replied with a sigh.

"What's going on?" Blayk asked as he entered the kitchen.

"Are you all right, sugar?" James asked as he, too, entered the small room.

"I'm sorry. I didn't mean to wake you all." Talia sighed again. Her eyes were glued to the three men standing before her in nothing but their formfitting boxer shorts. She slid her eyes over Chris's large, muscular thighs, past the growing bulge at his crotch, up his washboard abs, large pecs, and shoulders, and to his face. She began to tremble with desire at the heat she saw in his eyes.

Talia slid her eyes over Blayk and James as well. They were all so muscular and sexy, yet all so different from each other. She bit the inside of her cheek as her eyes wandered back down to their crotches. The underwear they had on left nothing to the imagination. They were built like stallions. Her pussy clenched, and she felt her panties dampen as her juices leaked out. She knew she was breathing rapidly, but she couldn't seem to control the responses of her own body. Her breath hitched in her throat as Chris stepped forward, until he was so close she could feel the heat emanating from his body. She tilted her neck back so she could see his eyes, and then she drowned in their depths.

Talia whimpered when she felt Chris's hands on her waist as he picked her up in his strong arms. He carried her a couple of feet and placed her on the counter. She still had to look up, but at least her neck wasn't as cricked as before. She held her breath as he slowly lowered his head to her, and then she moaned as his lips slid over hers. He was gentle with her, coaxing rather than demanding. He brushed his lips against hers, and then his tongue swept over her lower lip. She couldn't stand it anymore. She had wanted each of these men since the moment she had met them, and she allowed herself the luxury of giving in to her desires, if only for just this moment. She opened her mouth and reached up gripping his hair in her hands, and pulled him in closer.

The first taste of him and Talia was lost. She knew she would never be able to get enough. He tasted of mint, man, and desire. His tongue slid along hers, and she responded, twirling her own around his. She felt him scoop her up into his arms, one muscular forearm beneath her ass supporting her weight as he devoured her mouth. He was aggressive yet gentle. He took what he wanted, yet coaxed a response from her. She was on fire and knew there was only one way to put out the flames. She whimpered into his mouth as he explored every part of her. He tickled the roof of her mouth with his tongue, over her teeth and along the inside of her cheeks. She wrapped her legs around him and clung, never wanting to let him go. She sobbed with frustration when he slowed the kiss and finally removed his lips from hers.

"We have to stop now, darlin'. If we don't we are going to end up in bed with you," Chris panted.

Talia was pleased that he was just as affected as she was from the carnal kiss and shifted her aching cunt against his stomach. The move slid the silk of her panties over her sensitive clit, and she knew she didn't want this to end. Not now. Not yet. She wanted to feel what it was like to be loved by the three men claiming to be her mates. She knew she was probably playing with fire, but she needed their hands and mouths touching her so much that she threw caution to the wind.

"Take me to bed," Talia whispered, looking into Chris's eyes. His nostrils flared as he inhaled, and his pupils dilated. He was staring at her with such fire in the depths of his eyes that she felt singed by them.

"Talia, be very sure about this. If we take you to bed and love you, we will end up claiming you. Our beasts are going to take over while we are buried in that sweet body of yours," Chris stated, his voice deeper than usual with desire.

Talia looked over Chris's shoulder and saw Blayk and James staring at her with the same heated look as their brother. She wanted this. She wanted them to make love to her and claim her more than anything. She knew she couldn't walk away from them. She realized then all her words of leaving had been full of false bravado. There was no way in hell she could walk away. Not now, when she finally had a chance at love and happiness. She returned her gaze to Chris's and took a deep breath.

"Take me to bed," Talia repeated.

There was no coaxing this time. Chris slanted his mouth over hers and kissed the breath right out of her. His tongue pushed into her mouth, between her lips, as his large hands clutched at the globes of her ass. She whimpered as he made love to her mouth, and then she was lying on her back, his large body over hers, covering her with gentle pressure. He withdrew his lips from hers and licked his way down over her jaw, and he nibbled his way over her neck.

Talia arched her hips up as he pushed her large T-shirt up her body, his hands sliding over the skin of her belly. He didn't hesitate when he reached her breasts. He cupped her mound with his large hand and swept his thumb back and forth over the peak. She felt her breasts swell and her nipples pucker and harden, reaching out for more of the pleasurable sensations. She sobbed with frustration as he removed his hand and his body from over hers. She opened her eyes, and her pussy clenched, gushing more cream at the sight of Blayk and James standing at the end of the bed. They were totally naked, and they were fisting their large cocks, sliding their hands up and down the length of their shafts.

Chris reached for her with his large hands, helping her into a sitting position on the massive bed. He pulled her T-shirt up over her head and threw it aside. He hooked his thumbs into the waistband of her panties and pulled them down her legs and off her feet. She was totally nude, and she felt so small and feminine, but also powerful for the first time in her life. Chris got off the bed and held her eyes to his as he removed his boxer shorts. She couldn't contain her gasp of awe at the sight of his large cock springing out from the nest of hair between his muscular thighs. The man was huge. Her cunt clenched, aching to be filled by him.

Talia mewled in the back of her throat as the three men moved together, as if by some unspoken command. They got on the bed with her, Blayk and James at her sides and Chris on the end of the bed near her feet. Chris reached for her ankles and smoothed his palms up and down her shins and calves, gently separating her legs, making room for himself to sit between her now-splayed thighs.

"You are so sexy, little darlin'. The sight of your sweet little bare pussy has my balls aching. I have to taste you, Talia. I can smell your sweet cream and I want that cream coating my tongue," Chris said.

Talia whimpered, and then he was there, lying between her thighs. The first lick of his tongue was pure bliss. She bucked her hips up, her lips opening on a silent scream of pleasure. Blayk leaned down and covered her mouth with his. He swept his tongue into her mouth, and she dueled with him, tasting his masculine desire. One hand began to massage her breast, and she cried out into his mouth as she felt lips close around her other aching nipple. The mouth at her breast licked, nibbled, and sucked as the mouth on her pussy devoured. She sobbed out her pleasure and frustration as Blayk weaned his mouth from hers, but then she moaned with delight as he sucked at her breast.

Talia bucked her hips up into Chris's mouth as he fucked her with his tongue and then swept that moist muscle up through her folds and flicked it gently back and forth over her clit. Her womb felt so heavy with her liquid desire, and her pussy clamped down, trying to keep that tongue on her clit. Then she felt his finger rimming her pussy hole, and she was gone. Her womb coiled tight, and then she screamed as he plunged his thick finger into her sheath and she shot over the edge into rapture. Her arousal reached its pinnacle as he pumped his finger a couple of times, all the while massaging her sensitive nub with his tongue. Chris didn't stop until the last wave of her orgasm slowed and finally subsided.

"You taste so fucking good. I want to spend hours eating your pussy, but I have to have you now," Chris rumbled in a deep, breathless voice.

Talia opened her eyes and looked at Chris as she clutched the two heads at her breasts with her hands.

"I've never… That was so good," Talia panted.

"You've never what, baby?" Blayk asked as he lifted his head to look at her.

"I've never had an orgasm before," Talia mumbled.

"Oh, darlin', we are so gonna love making you come over and over again. Your ex was a bastard, Talia. As far as we are concerned you are still a virgin and it will be our delight to teach you everything about your own body," Chris said as he sat up between her legs.

"But I'm not a virgin. I wish I could give you that, but I can't," Talia stated wistfully.

"Sugar, we are your first real lovers. That motherfucker doesn't count. He was obviously only out for his own gratification, so he didn't show you what it was really like," James said then leaned down and took her mouth beneath his.

Talia kissed him with everything she had. Her heart filled up with joy and another unknown emotion. She felt tears prick behind her eyeballs as she kissed James until they were both breathless. He eased back when the need for oxygen became paramount.

Talia looked down her body when she felt Chris's cock against the entrance to her pussy. She lifted her hips up from the bed, begging him to fill her. He clasped her hips in his large hands as he eased his hard rod into her body. Her muscles stretched, allowing him entrance, and she sobbed as his wide head popped through. He held still, giving her time to adjust to his girth, and then he was pushing into her. She was so wet from her earlier orgasm that once he was past the tight muscles to her entrance, he slid in easily until he was buried in her balls-deep. He thrust a few times, letting her adjust and stretch as he massaged the walls of her cunt with his big dick.

She reached for him the same time he reached for her. He picked her up with ease until she was straddling his lap, impaled on his erection. She moaned as he slid another inch into her, until she could feel him butting up against her cervix. He cupped her chin with his hand and lifted her head to his. He bent down and took her mouth, the heat and carnality of the kiss making her pussy walls clench and release around his hard flesh. He grasped her buttocks in his large hands and kneaded her flesh, separating her until she felt cool air on the exposed skin of her puckered anus. She withdrew her mouth from Chris's and turned her head when she felt a wet tongue sliding between the cheeks of her ass and over her rosette. Blayk looked up at her and gave her a grin and a wink.

"What are you doing?" Talia asked, suddenly concerned.

"I'm just getting you nice and wet, baby. I'm preparing you so we can love you at the same time," Blayk replied.

"I don't think you should be doing that. It's not right."

"Did it feel good, Talia?" Blayk asked as he looked into her eyes.

"Well, yes."

"Then it's not wrong. If we do something you don't like then we'll stop. But if you like what we're doing to you then it's right. There is nothing wrong with the way we love you or you love us, unless you or we don't like it. Just relax and feel, baby. We want to make you feel good," Blayk stated and ducked down behind her again.

Talia couldn't contain her moan of pleasure as Blayk began to lick her ass again. He removed his mouth, and then she felt him pushing a finger against her skin. Her internal muscles clamped down on Chris's cock, and she wiggled, trying to get him to move within her. She heard the pop as a bottle was opened, and then cold, wet fingers massaged against the pucker of her anus. She closed her eyes and savored the sensations as Blayk eased a finger into her tight ass. She pushed her hips back, giving Blayk better access to her back entrance, and groaned as she felt him push two fingers into her body. There was a slight pinch and burn, but the little bite of pain only seemed to enhance her pleasure and arousal. She felt him spread his fingers wide, stretching her muscles as he pumped his digits in and out of her ass.

Talia had never realized just how sensitive her ass was until Blayk began paying attention to that particular part of her body. She was so hot. She wanted him to bury his cock into her body so he and Chris could love her, now. She felt a large, blunt object push against the pucker of her ass and knew Blayk was trying to gain entrance to her anus. She concentrated on trying to keep her muscles relaxed, but it wasn't an easy feat when her instinct was to clench. Blayk placed his hands on her waist and slid his large palms up to cup her breasts and tweak her nipples. His voice rumbling in her ear only made her burn hotter.

"The head of my cock's in your ass now, baby. Breathe in and out and try to relax. Yeah, that's it, Talia. God, you're so hot and tight. Use those muscles of yours and push me out. Fuck yeah, that's so good, baby."

Talia pushed her hips back as Blayk's cock slid into her ass, easing his way past the tight ring of muscles of her sphincter. She could feel her walls rippling along the two cocks now buried in her ass and cunt. She turned her head and sucked air into her lungs, her lips bumping on something hot and wet. She opened her eyes and looked up to see James kneeling in front of her, gripping his cock in his fist, the tip of his dick inches from her mouth. She didn't hesitate.

She opened her mouth and sucked him into her moist cavern. She twirled her tongue over the top of his dick, tasting the pre-cum leaking out of the small slit on top. She laved underneath his cock then sucked him down until he was touching the back of her throat. She hollowed her cheeks out as she glided up over his shaft, then sucked him in again.

"Jesus. Your mouth is lethal, sugar. I can already feel my balls tightening up. You are so fucking hot, Talia. Yeah, that feels so good." James groaned as she sucked and retreated over his hard dick.

Talia couldn't get enough now that she tasted him. She wanted him to fill her mouth with his cum, and she wanted to swallow it all down. She picked up the pace and reached over to massage and roll his balls gently in the palm of her hand.

Talia lost her rhythm as Chris withdrew his cock from her cunt until he was just resting in her body, and surged in again. As he pushed in, Blayk pulled out of her ass, and glided back in. They set up a slow rhythm of advance and retreat as she sucked, licked, and bobbed over James's cock. With each of the men counterthrusting, one of them filled her holes at all times. Her limbs were shaking, and liquid warmth traveled from her lower abdomen down to her pussy and her legs. Her internal muscles coiled tighter and tighter, and she knew she was getting close to climax. The sound of Chris's voice penetrated her passion-fogged mind.

"I want to claim you, darlin'. Talia, will you let us claim you as our mate?" Chris asked her.

Talia took her mouth from James's cock and turned her head to look up at Chris. His eyes were a glowing gold color, and she knew his beast was close to the surface. She didn't know if he would hurt her, but she was so fascinated by the three brothers, it was enough for her to risk getting hurt again. She only hoped she wasn't setting herself up for more pain by becoming involved with werewolves once more.

"Yes, claim me. Bite me. Fuck me," Talia yelled then sucked James's cock back into her mouth.

Her acceptance seemed to snap the control the three men had held over themselves. James clutched a handful of hair and began to gently pump his hips, sliding his cock in and out of her mouth. Chris and Blayk began to slam their hips into her as they shuttled their cocks in and out of her pussy and ass. Talia had never experienced so much pleasure. It consumed her and overwhelmed her. She heard James growl, and then he shouted.

"I'm gonna come, sugar. Swallow my seed, Talia."

Talia felt his cock pulse. She scraped her nails over his ball sac and then swallowed rapidly as he spewed his essence into the back of her throat and roared out his release. She sucked him off, making sure she licked him clean. And then she was there, on the precipice of nirvana.

Her breath froze in her throat, and she tilted her head back and screamed as pleasure wracked her body. Her toes curled and tingled, as did her legs. Her pelvic-floor muscles contracted, and her whole body trembled and shook as she reached climax and flew to the stars. Cream flooded from her body, and she coated Chris with her pussy juices. Chris yelled as he thrust his hips three, four more times, and he held his upper body still as he pumped her full of hot semen. She heard Blayk follow close behind as he groaned, slamming his hips up against her ass, and he, too, filled her full of his seed.

Talia flopped against Chris's chest, her muscles lax with satiation, and then tensed as she felt two mouths bite down on either side of her neck, and another above her right breast. White-hot pleasure/pain shot through her system, and she flew to the stars again. The orgasm seemed to go on forever, her body shaking and quaking as she flew with rapture. She had never felt anything like it before. She felt as if a circle formed and snapped closed as her mates claimed her for their own.

Chapter Five

"Hi, Michelle, Keira," Talia greeted.

Talia was in her element. She had been living with her mates for the last week and had never felt so cherished and loved. Not that any of her men had actually told her they loved her, but the way they treated her meant more to her than words ever would. She had been told she was loved before and then used as a punching bag to show just how much she was cared for. She didn't need to hear those three little words from her mates. They showed her in ways she had never seen before. They made sure she had food on her plate before she was able to do it. They cared and comforted her when she awoke night after night from her nightmares, and they talked to her. That meant more than anything. They treated her like an equal, not someone who was beneath them, and they made love to her every night. Her heart had never felt so full and safe, and she knew she loved her three Friess men with the whole of her heart and soul.

Talia smiled as she walked outside to meet Michelle, the queen and mate to the Alphas of the Friess Pack, and Keira, who was mated with her men's cousins. They were going shopping and were headed for the town of Aztec, as Talia only had a few clothes. Chris had given her his gold credit card and had told her not to worry about how much she spent, to enjoy her day, and she had every intention of doing just that.

Michelle drove the SUV. They were in the town of Aztec twenty minutes later, and she followed Michelle and Keira into a small boutique which looked like it only sold designer clothes. She watched as her two new friends flitted about the store chatting excitedly, but she baulked when she saw the price tag on a nice shirt. She didn't like the fact that she couldn't afford to spend money here, and she didn't feel right spending money that wasn't hers.

"Talia, get your ass over here, girl. You need to start picking out some clothes or we have orders to pick them out and buy them for you," Keira said with a smile her way. "I know how you feel about spending money that's not yours. There was a time that I was in the same boat you are. Even though I had a trust fund left to me by my parents, I couldn't touch it."

"Talia, your mates want you to get anything and everything you need. Don't worry about spending their money, honey. Your men are nearly as rich as King Midas. In fact all the men of the pack are filthy rich from all the properties they own, so don't you go worrying about spending their money. Now, what do think of this?" Michelle asked as she held up a royal-blue teddy.

"That is so gorgeous. I can see you in that. You will look so damn sexy," Talia stated as Michelle held up the lingerie.

"My thoughts exactly, but this color is for you. Go get some more clothes and try them on. We aren't leaving until you have a closet full of clothes and loads of underwear," Michelle said as she shoved the teddy at Talia.

"You guys are the best," Talia said in a voice thick with emotion as she took the teddy and then went on searching the racks.

By the time the three women left the shop, it felt like they had cleaned out the store of all its merchandise. Talia had several pairs of jeans, a couple of skirts with mix-and-match tops, two dresses, lingerie, and shoes to go with everything. They headed to the SUV, dumped their purchases, and then walked toward the small café across the street.

As Talia followed behind her two friends, she heard the squeal of tires on the road and turned her head toward the sound. The sight of a large dual-cab truck barreling toward her froze her in her tracks.

Then she sprang into action. She pushed Michelle and Keira out of the way just as the truck was upon them. She leaped and threw herself forward, landing on the opposite side of the road on her hands and knees. Her palms burned as she scraped her skin, and she felt a white-hot pain in her knee where she landed awkwardly. She looked up to see the taillights of the truck disappearing around a corner in the distance.

"Oh my God. Talia, are you all right?" Michelle asked as she helped her to her feet.

"Yeah, I'm fine," she replied but couldn't contain her wince as pain shot through her knee.

"Talia, you just saved us from being run over," Keira said as she placed her hands over the small bump of her belly. "What did the asshole think he was doing? Was he fucking blind?"

"I think they were after me," Talia stated as she limped across the pavement with the help of her new friends.

"What the hell does that mean?" Michelle asked with a scowl on her face.

"Obviously you haven't been told," Talia said as they entered the café.

"Told what?" Keira asked.

Talia explained to Michelle and Keira about her disastrous marriage, her hospitalization and divorce, and her flight from her ex-husband. "I think my ex may have found out where I am."

"But you're divorced," Michelle said. "What does he want with you now?"

Talia shrugged. "I found out he was after me and I didn't ask questions. He's crazy."

"Talia, you are so brave. Are you all right? Let me have a look at that knee," Keira said and held the door to the café open for her. She helped her to a seat and squatted down in front of her. "It's already beginning to heal, thank goodness. Now that your mates have claimed you, there is werewolf DNA flowing through your body, which enhances your healing ability. Michelle, call in for reinforcements," Keira said.

"Shit, do you think that's necessary? Nothing happened. We're all okay," Talia stated.

"I'm not willing to take any chances. What if that was your ex and he comes next time with a gun? Keira is pregnant, and I have a baby at home. I'm not leaving anything to chance," Michelle said, and Talia saw her pull her cell phone from her purse.

Talia tried to concentrate on Michelle and Keira, but she kept seeing that large truck bearing down on her and her friends. It was just pure dumb luck that Keira hadn't fallen over when she had pushed her. She wouldn't have been able to live with her conscience if she had hurt Keira, but most especially Keira's baby. She began to shake and knew she was reacting now that the adrenaline was leaving her system. She felt tears prick her eyes, and even though she tried to contain them, they spilled down over her cheeks. She had to leave. She couldn't stay here knowing she could get other innocent people hurt when it wasn't necessary.

She ignored the pain in her knee and jumped to her feet. She was at the door to the café before the two women could react, but she had forgotten that Keira was a werewolf. The other woman was at her side in moments, gripping her firmly by the arm and pulling her back to the table.

"You're not going anywhere. Where did you think you were going anyway? Your car isn't here and just think about how your mates will react if they find you gone. You're hurt and need attention and you have nowhere else to go," Keira said as she pushed Talia gently but firmly back into her seat.

"I can't do this. I can't stay here and see people I care about get hurt because of me. It's not right, Keira," Talia sobbed.

"No. What isn't right is thinking you can protect us when it's not necessary. You're the one they're after. You are the one who needs protection, Talia. You can't spend the rest of your life on the run. I know what that's like, I tried that myself. You have to take a stand and fight for what you've got, girlfriend. You can't let this bastard win. You are safer with us and the pack. Don't you know they will protect you with their lives?" Keira asked.

"That's what I'm scared of. I don't want anyone getting hurt because of me. It's not fair and it's not right," Talia sobbed.

"Was it right for that freak to use you as a punching bag and a sexual object?" Keira asked and held up her hand to stop Talia from interrupting. "Don't you dare deny what he did to you. We know what it's like to be loved by your mates. What he did to you was wrong on so many levels. It wasn't your fault, Talia. None of it was your fault and neither was the fact he nearly hurt us when he was trying to get to you. Nearly doesn't count," Keira smiled. "Oh shit, I think I just creamed my panties. The cavalry have arrived."

Talia laughed through her tears at Keira's off-the-wall statement, and turned to look out the window. Her breath hitched and her pussy dripped as the sight of nine tall, sexy, handsome men getting out of trucks, but her reaction was only for the three men who had already claimed her heart.

Talia watched as Jonah, Mikhail, and Brock Friess pinned their eyes on Michelle. Greg, Jake, and Devon Domain only had eyes for Keira, and as she slid her eyes to the left she saw that Chris, Blayk, and James were looking at her. She could see their worry and concern, but she could also see the fire in their eyes as they stared at her. The men were beside her moments later. She gasped as she was plucked from her seat and lifted over the back, and then she was in Chris's arms. He cradled her against his chest as he looked down at her.

"Are you okay, darlin'? Did that bastard hurt you?"

"No, I'm fine. Just a little scraped up is all."

"Where are you hurt, baby?" Blayk asked from her side.

"Just my hand and knees, but they're already healing."

"Let me see, sugar," James said. He took her hands in his, and he winced at her scraped, bloody palms. He released her hands and knelt down. He pushed up her jeans, being careful not to hurt her, and he grimaced at the deep cut in her right knee. Blayk was at his side examining her wounds as well.

"We need to get you home, baby. I want to clean these up for you," Blayk said.

"Okay," Talia replied with a sigh and snuggled into Chris. It felt so good to be in his arms as her three men fussed over and cared for her. She hadn't been cared for in so long. She looked over Chris's shoulder as he carried her out of the café and saw Michelle and Keira being carried out behind her. She didn't care that the other patrons gawked at the scene they made. She was happy and safe with her men here with her. She was looking forward to going home.

Talia was surprised when Chris let her sit in her own seat in the truck then figured he probably wanted her safe and secure with her safety belt on. She sighed and closed her eyes as James slowed the truck and turned into the driveway of the Friess pack house. She was feeling rather tired and drained after the events of the day. She wanted to shower and change and maybe take a nap, but first she would let Blayk tend her wounds. He was a doctor after all, and she knew he would need to feel as if he had taken care of her.

She opened her eyes when James pulled the truck to a stop. Chris was out of the vehicle and at her door before she could blink. He unbuckled her belt and lifted her up into his arms once more.

"I can walk, you know," Talia said gently.

"I know you can, darlin'. Why risk hurting yourself when you have me to carry you? I'll help you with your bath and then Blayk can fix you up. All right?"

"Okay, but I'm not even hurt bad, just scraped up a little," Talia said, hoping to placate Chris.

"We should never have let you go out alone, Talia. One of us should have been with you so we could protect you. We knew there was a possibility that bastard would find you. This should never have been able to happen. We could have prevented it," Chris stated.

Talia could tell by the tone of his voice that he was berating himself. She had never had anyone so concerned for her welfare before, and the knowledge that he and his brothers worried for her filled her heart with joy.

"You can't be with me twenty-four hours a day seven days a week. It's just not possible. It wasn't your fault, Chris. I knew the risks as well, but I was so excited about going out with Michelle and Keira, the thought of being found and attacked never even entered my mind. So if anyone is to blame, it is me," Talia said.

"No, darlin'. It's our job and need as your mates to make sure you are safe. From now on you don't go anywhere without one of us by your side."

"Won't that be difficult since you guys are the security around this place? I know that's not all you do, but I know you have responsibilities to keep the pack safe."

"Yes, darlin', we do have responsibilities and our first priority is to you. You are our mate, Talia. We can't lose you. We have waited for you for a long time," Chris said.

Talia sighed and rested her head on Chris's shoulder. She hoped she had hidden her disappointment at him not telling her what she wished to hear. She didn't understand why she needed to hear her mates tell her they loved her. She knew she was in love with them, but she wasn't sure if she could say the words out loud yet. How could she expect to hear those three words from her mates when she couldn't say them herself?

Talia pushed those thoughts to the back of her mind. She wondered if it had been her ex after her, or if it had just been a coincidence. The windows on the vehicle had been too dark for her to see through, and everything had happened so quickly, she hadn't been able to get a look at the license plate. Could it really have been Paul in that truck? She didn't know anyone besides her mates and some of the pack members. She hadn't been here long enough. She knew there were probably members of the Friess Pack she hadn't even encountered yet. There were always people coming and going at all times of the day and night.

Talia lifted her head as Chris carried her into the massive bathroom. He sat her on the vanity and turned on the faucets on the tub. He turned back to her and was about to help her remove her clothes when Blayk and James entered the room.

"Blayk, you should go and check on Keira. I had to push her out of the way of the truck so she wouldn't get hurt," Talia said with concern.

"Did she fall?" Blayk asked.

"Well, no, but that's not the point. She's pregnant, so you should check on her."

Talia became a little disconcerted as Blayk stood staring at her, but his eyes were unfocused. She saw a smile cross and face, and then he looked into her eyes.

"Keira's fine, baby," Blayk said.

"How can you know that? You haven't even examined her," Talia asked with a frown.

"I know because I just spoke to Greg through our telepathic link. He says Keira and the baby are just fine."

"You can talk to each other in your heads?" Talia asked incredulously.

"Yeah, baby. I thought you would have known that," Blayk stated.

"Well, no. It seems there are a lot of things I didn't know." She had never really been part of her ex's pack. No one ever told her anything.

"Don't worry about it now, darlin'. Let's get you cleaned up," Chris said and pulled her top over her head by the hem.

Talia was naked and in the tub moments later. Chris got in with her and began to wash her. The cut on her knee and the abrasions on her palms stung like a bitch when she first got in the water, but when it eased after a few moments, she savored the warmth relaxing her aching muscles. Once she was clean Chris picked her up and handed her over to Blayk. He held her steady while James dried her off, being careful not to touch her injuries. Blayk wrapped her up into a large bathrobe, and she giggled when the arms covered her hands and the hem pooled on the floor around her feet. He bent down and picked her up and carried her to Chris's bedroom.

"Just sit tight, baby. I'm going to clean you up," Blayk stated.

Talia smiled as Blayk turned and reached for a black bag she hadn't seen resting on a chair off to the side of the room. James walked over to her and began to roll up the sleeves on the borrowed robe. She inhaled the scent and knew the robe was Chris's. She held still while Blayk cleaned her wounds with alcohol swabs, and then he covered the gash on her knee with a large bandage. She was glad he had covered the worst wound as she didn't want to get blood on the quilt or sheets. Even though the gash was healing rapidly, a little blood still seeped from it. She covered her mouth and yawned. Her eyelids felt heavy, and she wanted to take a nap.

Talia smiled when Chris entered the room fully dressed again. He must have seen she was tired because he walked over to her and picked her up. He held her in one strong arm and pulled back the covers. He placed her on the bed and covered her, making sure she was warm.

"Take a nap, darlin'. You'll feel better after sleeping for a couple of hours. We have a few things to take care of, but we'll be here when you wake up," Chris said.

Talia felt herself drifting off to sleep, secure with the knowledge that her men were close by and keeping her safe.

Chapter Six

Chris walked into the large study at the back of the house, his brothers following. He looked at the concerned faces of his three Alphas and knew it was going to be a long afternoon.

"How is your mate?" Jonah asked.

"She's a little banged up, but she's okay," Chris replied.

"Did she see who was driving the truck or get the license plates?"

"No. She said the windows were too darkly tinted to see anyone and that things happened too fast for her to get the plate. Did Michelle or Keira see the truck?"

"No," Jonah replied. "They said all the heard was a screech of tires and then Talia pushed them out of the way."

"Thank God they're all right. I don't know if it was Talia's ex," Chris said as he took a seat. His brothers were standing at the back of the room listening intently. He had seen them before he sat down.

"From now on, none of the women in this pack go anywhere without one of her mates by her side. We take care of our own."

"Yes, Jonah. We'd already spoken about not letting Talia go anywhere without one of us with her. We don't plan to let her out of our sight when she's not in the house," Chris said.

"Good, then that's settled. See what else you can learn from Talia about the pack she was with. We need to know all we can about them, and I want you to see what you can dig up on their Alpha," Jonah stated.

Chris rose from the chair and headed to his desk and laptop in the security room. He and his brothers had a lot of work to do.

A couple of hours later Chris stretched as he stood up. He had found little to no information on Paul Rogan and his brother, the Alpha. He had a feeling they were looking in the totally wrong direction, but he had no idea where else to look. Chris strode from the room, leaving his brothers to look for possible enemies. He intended to see if Talia was awake. The need to feel her small, slender body against his after this morning's fiasco was pulling at him.

He opened the door to his room just as Talia rolled over to her back and opened her eyes. Her cheeks were flushed from sleep, and her hair was tousled and her eyes sleepy. She had never looked so sexy. She smiled at him as he walked to the bed and sat at her side.

"Hey, darlin'. Do you feel better?"

"Yes, thanks. I can't believe how long I slept," Talia replied, and she glanced at the clock on the bedside table.

"You're catching up on all the sleep you missed out on while you were on the run," Chris said as he gently pushed her hair back, away from her face.

"Maybe, but I never was one to take a nap," Talia replied.

"You have no idea how sexy you are, do you, darlin'?" Chris whispered as he leaned down over her, bracketing her body with his arms on either side of her.

"I'm not sexy." Talia whispered her reply.

"Oh yes you are. Let me show you just how sexy you are, darlin'," Chris said and leaned down to kiss her.

Chris groaned against her lips at the first taste of her. He knew he would never be able to get enough of her. He swept his tongue into her mouth, tasting every nook and cranny as he gathered her up in his arms. He pulled her onto his lap and slid his hand beneath her robe. He moaned as her little nipple stabbed against the palm of his hand while he kneaded her soft flesh. The whimpering sounds she made as he plucked her hard peak between his thumb and finger made his cock jerk against the zipper of his jeans and his balls ache. He wanted to strip down to his skin and sink his cock into her warm, wet depths. He slowed the kiss and began to nibble and lick his way across her jaw to her ear. He nipped at her earlobe and flicked his tongue into her ear canal. She mewled with pleasure and wrapped her arms around his neck, pulling him in closer to her.

Chris undid the belt of her robe and separated the material. He lifted his head and looked down at her exposed breasts and body. He could smell her cream and wanted to lay her down on the bed and feast on her. So that was exactly what he did. He removed the robe from her body and gently placed her on the bed. He rose to his feet, shucked his clothes, and crawled up between her legs. He smoothed his hands up the inside of her thighs and sighed when she opened to him. He lay down on the mattress between her thighs and lowered his head to her bare pussy. He licked over her clit and grasped her hips in his hands to hold her still when she bucked under him. His cock pulsed and throbbed against the quilt with eagerness as he scented her arousal.

He sucked her little engorged nub into his mouth and slipped two fingers into her cunt. He nibbled and laved her as he pumped his digits in and out of her pussy. He loved listening to the sounds she made as he pleasured her. He heard the bedroom door open and knew James and Blayk had joined them. He heard the rustling sounds as his brothers removed their clothes, but didn't stop what he was doing. He looked up along the length of Talia's petite body and groaned at the sight of her. Her neck was arched, her head thrown back, and she was flushed from her breasts all the way up to her forehead. Her hair was spilling around her shoulders as her head thrashed back and forth on the pillow.

Chris withdrew his mouth and hands from her body. He couldn't wait any longer. He wanted, needed to feel her wet warmth envelop him. He moved up between her thighs, waited until she looked at him, and then began to push his hard cock into her cunt. He held her hips firmly as she tried to impale herself on his dick, but made sure not to hurt her. He eased his way into her sheath with slow, short digs, until he was buried balls-deep.

"Are you okay, darlin'?" Chris asked as he held still.

"Yes. Please, Chris."

"Please what, Talia?"

"Please move," Talia whimpered.

"Okay, darlin'. I'll give you what you need," Chris rasped out.

He began to move then. He thrust his hips slowly, forging his way in and out of her body. He had never felt anything that even compared to making love with his mate. He was in bliss as his cock slid in and out of her wet cunt. He could feel every ripple and flutter of her internal muscles and knew he would never be able to get enough of her. He was aware of James and Blayk lying on either side of Talia as they kissed her and played with her nipples, but he concentrated on giving his mate pleasure.

"You feel so good, darlin'. Your pretty little cunt is so hot and wet and tight. I love making you feel good, Talia. Your eyes get glazed when we pleasure you. Your skin is so soft and sweet. I love the taste of your cunt. I could spend hours eating out that pretty little pussy," Chris said on a groan as he thrust his hips forward. "Does that feel good, darlin'?"

"Yes," Talia replied and then sobbed out her pleasure. "I need more."

"Tell us what you need, baby," Blayk said.

"I want all of you. I need you to love me at the same time," Talia cried out with desperation.

"Are you sure, sugar?" James asked. "We don't want to hurt you after this morning."

"I'm fine. I need all of you."

Chris stopped pumping his hips and pulled Talia up onto his lap. He moved to the edge of the bed with his feet on the floor, and lifted her up off his cock. He turned her around so her back was to his front. He placed her legs over his and spread his thighs wide, giving James access to Talia's pussy. He watched his brother lean over and kiss their mate, and then he stood up, bent his knees, and began to penetrate Talia's sheath. Chris moved out of the way when James lifted Talia into his arms. His brother lay down on the bed on his back, taking Talia with him so she was lying on top of James.

Chris moved up behind Talia after he grabbed a tube of lube from the bedside, and he kissed along her spine as he began to massage the cool gel into her anus while James held her ass cheeks open. He was careful and gentle with her as he penetrated her canal, stretching her muscles out in preparation for him to fuck her ass. When he was satisfied that her ass was relaxed and loose he began to push his cock into her anus. He groaned as the ring of muscles clamped down on his erection. She was so hot and tight, and he was in danger of climaxing too soon. He sighed when he felt Talia push back against him, easing the tightness around his rod, and he was able to surge forward gently until his balls were flush against her skin. He held still, giving her time to get used to being so full of cock.

"Are you okay, baby?" Blayk asked.

"Yes," Talia moaned.

"Will you suck on my cock, Talia? I need to feel that sweet mouth of yours wrapped around me." Blayk groaned.

Chris didn't hear Talia answer, but he saw her reach out and wrap her hand around Blayk's dick, and then she took his cock into her mouth. Chris had never seen a sexier sight. He couldn't hold still any longer. He began to move his hips backward and forward, making love to his mate. He loved the sensations of her flesh sliding along the length of his shaft. He moved in countermotion with James as they began to love their woman in earnest.

Chris wrapped his arms around Talia and filled his palms with her breasts. He pinched and tweaked her nipples as he fucked into her ass. He loved the little sounds she made as she sucked and loved on Blayk's cock. He could feel her internal muscles coiling tighter and tighter and knew she was close to reaching climax. He leaned down and nibbled on the side of her neck, and then he licked over the mark he'd made when he claimed her.

Talia screamed around Blayk's dick as she shot up and over the edge and her body shook and clamped down on his hard erection. He couldn't hold back anymore. He shuttled his cock in and out of her body, his balls drew up tight, and he roared as he joined his mate in rapture. He was vaguely aware of his brothers reaching their own releases, and he held Talia in his arms as the last waves of their orgasmic bliss faded away.

Chris slowly withdrew his rapidly diminishing cock from her ass and kissed her shoulder. He strode to the bathroom, cleaned himself off, and was back in moments with a warm, wet washcloth to clean his mate up. He lifted her off James and gently laid her down. He lifted her leg, cleaned her, and then got onto the bed to cuddle with her. He had never felt so content, as when he was holding Talia in his arms or loving on her. She made him feel so complete, and he vowed to protect her with his life.

Chapter Seven

Talia was pulling weeds from the vegetable garden when she saw a shadow looming over her. She turned her head and rolled her eyes mentally when she saw James standing nearby.

Talia had been living with her mates for a few weeks now, and no one else had attempted to hurt her or get to her. Not that they'd had much of a chance. At least one of her mates was with her nearly all the time, and even though she appreciated their vigilance, she was becoming sick and tired of not being able to make a cup of coffee without getting the third degree. Michelle and Keira were just as annoyed as she was. Talia had become bored, and she had started working in the garden every day. She knew it wasn't necessary, but she needed to do something from keeping herself from going stir-crazy.

"You do know you don't have to do that, don't ya, sugar? Jonah employs someone to come and take care of the gardens," James stated.

"I know, but I've never been one to sit around on my ass doing nothing. At least I'm keeping myself occupied," Talia replied.

"What do you want to do with your time, sugar? We want you to be happy," James said.

"Well, actually, I'm enjoying what I'm doing now. Jonah doesn't need to hire someone to look after the gardens. I like gardening," Talia stated.

"You can't do all of it by yourself, Talia. The gardens are too much for one person."

"Yeah, I suppose you're right. Why don't you give me a hand?" she suggested.

"Um, gardening is not really my thing, sugar," James replied. Talia had to bite her lip to keep from laughing at the pained look on James's face.

"Gee, really? I would never have guessed," she replied facetiously and burst out laughing.

"You're such a smart-ass. I love it when you're sassy," James said and gave her a heated look.

"Don't even think about it, buster. I have too much I want to get done here. Don't you have work to do?"

"Yeah, always. I just wanted to check on you."

"You don't need to, you know. I'm perfectly safe. No one can get in without anybody knowing, so you don't have to keep checking on me."

"I know, but we like to make sure you're all right."

"You guys are so sweet to be concerned for me. I never had that before."

"That's 'cos you weren't mated before," James replied and he walked toward her. He leaned down and kissed her gently on the lips and straightened again. He gave her a wink and tapped her on the ass and walked back toward the house.

Talia sighed as she watched James disappear inside. She felt so loved and cherished by Chris, Blayk, and James. She'd never known that sort of respect before. She was already half in love with them. They had crept in beneath her skin and into her heart when she hadn't been looking. She didn't know what to make of all the mated men in the pack. They were all so courteous and solicitous to their women.

When she had lived with the Rogan Pack, all the males had treated the women like dirt. They were told what to do all they time and had no say in what went on in the pack. She'd often wondered why the females had put up with that. But she knew they had been too scared to make a stand or to leave. The men of Rogan Pack were such assholes. She shivered and hoped she never had to deal with any of them again.

Talia pushed her thoughts aside and got back to work. Once she'd finished weeding the vegetable garden, she was going to work on the flower beds, and they were vast. The garden surrounded the whole house and the grounds. She was so intent on what she was doing that the sound of footsteps behind her didn't register. She was kneeling on the grass beside a flower bed when she noticed a shadow over her. She half turned, but she wasn't quick enough. She felt a prick in the side of her neck, and then her world began to get blurry. She tried to call out, but a large hand clamped down over her mouth, muffling the sound. She tried to hold on to consciousness, but she knew she had been drugged and couldn't fight off the effect on her system. Her eyelids slid closed as she felt herself being lifted from the ground, and then she knew no more.

* * * *

Blayk couldn't find Talia anywhere. He had been searching for ten minutes, and there was no sign of her in the gardens. He sniffed where her scent was the most prominent near one of the flower gardens, fifty yards from the house, and he caught the scent of a human male.

"Talia's not out here. She's missing. Check the house. I'm going to change forms and see if I can find her," Blayk explained to his brothers mentally. He removed his clothes and called on his wolf, and felt his human pull back. He landed on his hands and knees as his muscles and bones began to reshape and contort. The familiar sound of his bones cracking and his joints popping as his wolf formed comforted him. He bent his head to the ground and sniffed as his wolf took over and followed his mate's scent.

"I only checked on her a little while ago. Where the hell could she be?" James asked.

"*I don't know, bro. But I don't like this. I have a bad feeling,*" Blayk replied.

"*She's not in the house. Have you found her trail?*" Chris asked.

"*Fuck. The back perimeter has been breached. It looks like someone has tampered with the camera and we're getting a continuous loop feed. Shit. Get the others to make sure their mates are safe. The lock on the far gate has been cut and the alarm has been disabled. Whoever it is knows what they were doing,*" Blayk said. He could smell the scent of another werewolf on the ground near the camera. The wires to the camera had been cut and were being fed by another close to the ground.

"*We'll be there in a minute. All the other females are safe. Can you pick up on who it was that took her?*" Chris asked.

"*Only that it was a werewolf male in human form. Whoever it was had a large car or truck waiting for them. This was planned. How the hell, are we supposed to find her if we don't know who we're looking for?*" Blayk snarled his question.

"*We're going to need help on this. James, get Greg, Jake, and Devon to see what they can find. We need to search through Talia's things and see if we can find out anything about that Rogan Pack. It has to be them. Every other wolf within a hundred-mile radius has better sense than to trespass here. Blayk, get your ass back to the house. I'm going to need your help going through her stuff,*" Chris commanded.

Blayk was back at the house five minutes later. He stopped to pull his clothes back on, and then he bounded up the stairs. He found Chris in the spare bedroom going through Talia's things thoroughly. He walked over to the chest of drawers and began to pull her things out.

"Don't bother with the new stuff, but look over everything she brought with her. I have a gut feeling we will find what we're looking for in her things. Make sure you examine all her clothes as well as any makeup containers," Chris explained.

"What do you think we're looking for?" Blayk asked.

"I don't know. It's just a hunch I'm going on, but wolves like Talia's ex like to mark their women. They're no better than property to those men. But we may not find anything," Chris replied.

Blayk got to work. He pushed aside Talia's new things and concentrated on what she had brought with her. He looked in books and book covers. He pulled makeup compacts and eye-shadow containers apart. He ran his finger over the seams of her clothes and dug into pockets. He found nothing. He picked her purse up from the top of the dresser and tipped out the contents. He pulled her lipstick apart, and emptied her wallet and ran his fingers over the material. He picked up her license, and his finger caught on a small bulge. He turned it over and saw where it had been cut. Something had been inserted into the plastic.

"I think I just found your hunch," Blayk told Chris. "Her license has been tampered with."

"Bring it down to the office and let's see what we've got," Chris said.

Blayk led the way down the stairs and into the back room he and his brothers used as an office. He sat down at his desk, opened the drawer, and pulled out a small penknife. He carefully cut around the bulge beneath the plastic of Talia's license and peeled the plastic away. There was a small circuit sitting on the lower sheet of plastic. He recognized what it was and retrieved a card from the desk drawer. The card slotted into the smart card reader on his laptop.

He opened the file, and what he found on the screen in front of him blew his mind. If anyone ever got ahold of the information he had, the lives of werewolves as they knew them would be changed forever.

"Holy shit. Jonah," Blayk called out, knowing his Alpha would hear him due to the wolves' enhanced hearing abilities. "You'd better get in here and see this."

"What have you got?" Jonah asked when he entered the room.

Blayk was glad to see Jonah's brothers, Mikhail and Brock, as well as their cousins Greg, Jake, and Devon following Jonah.

"I found a circuit between two layers of plastic on Talia's license. What we have here is a formula on how to create the DNA strand of a werewolf. I'll bet whoever created this," Blayk said, indicating the computer monitor, "has our mate."

"Fuck. This could be disastrous if it got out. We could have werewolves running around creating havoc everywhere," Jonah growled out.

"Or even worse, I can just see it now. We'd have humans trying to kill all of our kind and scientists wanting to dissect us, in the name of science of course," Blayk said with a sigh of frustration.

"Do you think you can find out where this came from?" Jonah asked him.

"Well, I'm definitely going to try. Our mate's life depends on it," Blayk said with steely determination. He was going to find the bastard who had taken their mate if it was the last thing he did.

"Let me know when you find something," Jonah stated. "No one is to enter or leave the grounds. As of now we are in lockdown."

"Yes, Alpha," Blayk replied at the same time his brothers did. He planned to work all through the night with his brothers' help. There had to be something on this chip to indicate who had put the data here, and Blayk had every reason to think that person was Talia's ex. Finding more about the chip's maker would help them find her.

Blayk was thankful for the pot of coffee and the fact he was a werewolf with enhanced strength and stamina, as he and his brothers worked well into the early hours of the morning. He knew they were close to finding out who had made the werewolf DNA program and was eager to find the source. He had another of his security programs searching for any information he could find. He had used two others before and hadn't found anything. He was tired, frustrated, and worried about Talia. He wanted to change into his beast form and kill the bastard who had taken her, but he knew he had to be patient. Besides, he had no idea where to start looking just yet.

He walked out of the office intending to brew another pot of coffee, but the sound of his brother's voice called him back.

"We've got him, Blayk," Chris called. "It's that bastard ex of hers, all right. Check out the screen."

Blayk hurried over to the desk and looked. It seemed Paul Rogan was in deep with the mob. The screen showed information from his Swiss bank account indicating he had been taking payment from the leader of one of the largest drug cartels in the country, Tony Picotti.

The American Media had been rife with reports of Picotti's involvement in murder, kidnapping, rape, and countless other horrific offenses, but law enforcement hadn't been able to pin any proof on the evil bastard. If he got hold of the formula for werewolf DNA, then their kind could end up in deep shit.. Blayk felt chilled to the bone as he read the screen. Paul must have decided to do a little investigating himself, because there was a detailed itinerary of drug shipments as well as names and address of those involved in the drug trade.

"Paul was trying to cover his ass," Blayk said. "He's gathered information the Feds would love to get hold of. Let's make a copy and send what we have here to the Bureau, that way our conscience is clear in regards to the drug-trafficking monster, Picotti.

"See if you can pull up this asshole's address from the Internet. We need to study the layout of Paul's property so we can get in without being detected."

"I'm already on it," Chris said, typing furiously.

"James, see if you can find out how many are in their pack. We need to know how many men to take with us," Blayk stated.

"He's got a property a couple of hours away. Wanna bet that's where our girl is?" Chris asked. "Oh, and he has a dual-cab truck as well as an SUV registered in his name. I'll bet he was the fucker who tried to run the women down."

"Bastard! I'd count on it. I'm going to prepare my medical bag. I want to make sure I have everything I need, just in case. It's only a couple of hours till sunrise. We'll head out soon as we have everything ready and then we get our Alphas and our other cousins to come with us." Blayk stood to go, feeling grim at the task ahead of them. "We don't know what we'll really be up against until we get there."

Chapter Eight

Talia woke up with a mouth feeling like it was stuffed with cotton wool and what felt like a jackhammer pounding inside her skull. She opened her eyes to a slit and looked around the room. She remembered the prick in her neck and hands on her, then nothing. The room was bereft of any furniture but the bed she lay on. Frayed drapes covered the window, and the air smelled stale and damp. The room wasn't familiar to her, but the scents she could smell were. Her ex had found her. The stench of Paul Rogan permeated the air.

She shut her eyes when she heard footsteps outside the closed bedroom door and prayed to God he would still think she was asleep. He obviously didn't care one way or the other. The footsteps grew louder as the door opened, and the smell of Paul suddenly intensified. Talia screeched with pain as he grabbed her hair and pulled her up from the bed. She clawed at his hand with her nails, but he didn't let go.

"Welcome back, wife! Did you honestly think you could avoid me forever? You always were a dumb bitch. You belong to me, Talia, and I am going to make sure you stay by my side. Those wolves you've been fucking are dead meat. I always knew there was a slut buried underneath that innocent façade," Paul snarled at her.

"What do you want with me? I'm not your wife, we're divorced," Talia yelled as she continued to struggle.

"I don't give a shit about what a piece of paper says. You belong to me. Not that I want to fuck you or anything. I just need the chip you stole from me."

"What the hell are you talking about?" Talia cried out as he tugged on her hair.

"Oh, that's right. You were too dumb to know what was going on right underneath your nose. I have been working with some people to create a serum that changes humans to werewolves." He offered an evil grin. "Would you like to try it?"

"What? Are you insane? You can't go around changing people to werewolves. Think of the chaos that would cause."

"Yes, chaos! I am going to create the biggest pack in the whole world. I will be the ruler of them all," Paul stated with an evil grin on his face.

"What does your brother think of what you're doing? He won't let you take away his role as Alpha."

"No, he won't. He's no longer alive. I am now the Alpha of the Rogan Pack, and my pack will rule the world."

"You know you're insane, right?" Talia asked. She wished she hadn't let her tongue run away with her when his open palm landed on her cheek. The fire in her cheek brought tears to her eyes, and she felt her knees buckle. If he hadn't been holding on to her hair, she would have fallen to the floor.

"I'm not insane. I am a visionary," Paul ranted, spittle hitting her face as he went off in his own little world. "I can just imagine having all those people kneeling at my feet. I have plotted and planned this for years. I have even gathered information on the leader of the largest drug cartel on the planet and have him beneath the heel of my boot. Do you know what it's like to have that type of hold over someone? No, of course you don't. You're too dumb and innocent."

"What about the rest of the pack? They aren't going to like finding out you killed their precious Alpha."

"I don't give a shit what they think. Oh, ah, ah, ah, you're a naughty little wife, aren't you, Talia? Do you think I don't know what you're trying to do? I know you're trying to distract me. It won't work. Now, where is your driver's license?"

"I don't have it." Talia was bewildered. Her head throbbed. Why would he want her driver's license?

Paul shook her a little, making her wince. "You little slut!" All at once he looked panicky. "If anyone else gets that chip…"

"What chip?" Talia winced again when he glared at her, but she added, "You're not making any sense."

"I left a bit of information with you, my dear wife. For safekeeping. I wouldn't want it getting into any other hands. But then you left. You won't escape me again, you little whore. Now let's see how you enjoy becoming my own little bitch," Paul said and began to pull her out of the bedroom by her hair.

Talia knew she had to escape him. The man was insane. She didn't want to become a werewolf. Keira had told her how humans were changed, and she didn't want to endure the agony of having her guts ripped to shreds. She fought against him, but she was no match for his strength. He pulled her so hard and moved so quickly she had trouble keeping her feet beneath her. Her head hurt as he tugged her by the hair, but she kept on fighting.

They reached the top of a staircase, and Talia knew her chance had arrived. This was the only option she had, and she was going to go down fighting. She used the last of her waning strength and dug the heel of one foot into the floor for leverage. With the other foot, she tripped Paul. Then she slammed her whole body into him.

Paul teetered for a moment, and then he lost his balance. He began to fall, and she tried to pull back so she wouldn't go with him, but his grip on her hair was too strong. She screamed as she went tumbling down the long stairs with him. They rolled with unstoppable momentum. Her body smacked on top of Paul's, and then the stairs slammed into her back. Talia heard a sickening crack, and then blinding pain radiated up from beneath her chin into her jaw and head. She literally saw stars, and then she was totally blind. She slid down into the beckoning black abyss.

* * * *

Chris was silent as he drove the truck. The knot of fear and anxiety which had been in his gut since the moment he and his brothers had found out that Talia was missing got bigger with each passing hour she was gone. They were headed toward Marvel in Colorado, which was just an hour or so across the border from Aztec, New Mexico. His Alpha cousins, Jonah, Mikhail, and Brock, were following behind in their own truck as were his other cousins, Greg, Jake, and Devon. They planned to storm the large country house and leave no one standing. He had studied the plans of the house and grounds for hours, until he knew he could move around without having to think. He knew where all the bedrooms were, the kitchen, the study, and every other room in between. He knew where the garage and garden shed were situated, and he knew the security system would be a piece of cake to bypass. So why was he feeling so unsettled? The only reason he could come up with was because Talia was in danger.

He vowed to never let her out of his sight again. The thought of not having her with him for the rest of his life tore through his heart. He loved his mate so much and knew his brothers felt the same. The thought of her in the clutches of her ex was just too horrific to bear. He slowed the truck and took the exit from the freeway. It wouldn't be long now before he and his brothers had their woman back in their arms and in their bed. He glanced in the rearview mirror and saw the other two trucks traveling close behind. Pulling onto a quiet road, he slowed even more and traversed the small Colorado town. He pulled the truck to a stop five hundred yards from the Rogan property and got out.

Chris stood with his brothers until his six cousins joined them. He pushed his fear and anxiety to the back of his mind and silently led the way down the road. He made sure to keep out of sight of the windows once he had the property in his view. He and his cousins communicated through their wolves, knowing they were secure since it was a Friess Pack link. He and his brothers took the front door, while Jonah and Mikhail took the back. The rest of the men split up to either side of the house, covering all exits and entries.

Chris didn't bother trying the door to see if it was open. He kicked it in. The sound of the wood frame splintering was loud and echoed through the silence. He rushed through the door, his brothers at his back, and froze with shock and fear. He felt sick to his stomach when he saw Talia in a heap on the floor next to a man. He was glad Blayk was there because he couldn't seem to get his body to move. Blayk rushed past him and knelt down, placing a finger against Talia's neck to feel her pulse. His waited in terror and dread for Blayk to look at him. His knees nearly buckled when he heard his brother's words.

"She's alive. Chris, call for the paramedics while I check her over," Blayk commanded.

Chris stood over Talia and his brothers as James helped Blayk with their mate. She had a cut beneath her chin, a swollen, bruised cheek and a fat, lacerated lip, but she was breathing. He looked dispassionately at the man lying on the floor next to his mate. His neck was twisted at an odd angle, his eyes were wide open, and he wasn't breathing. The bastard was dead.

Chris heard sirens in the distance fifteen minutes later. He could tell by the way Blayk was frowning at Talia that he was worried about something, but Chris knew he would do everything he could to see Talia had the best possible medical care.

While his brothers had looked after their mate, his Alphas and cousins had searched the place for any incriminating evidence in regards to their species. They had found a lot of stuff down in a hidden basement and were pleased find the files on werewolf DNA had all been stored on the computer. Brock had copied the files onto a USB stick and then wiped the hard drive clean, removed it, and destroyed it.

He watched as Talia was loaded carefully onto a stretcher and carried into the ambulance. Blayk climbed in the back. He would let him and James know which hospital they drove Talia to. The local sheriff had arrived, and so had the coroner. Chris knew it was going to be a long day. He didn't want to have to deal with the local authorities, but he had no choice.

Three hours later Chris finally pulled his truck into the parking lot of the hospital in Durango, Colorado. He was bone tired since he hadn't slept a wink the night before, but he had to see Talia. Blayk had sent him and James periodic text messages letting them know that Talia's condition hadn't changed, but he needed to see her for himself. He entered through the double front doors to the medium-size hospital and hurried down the long corridor. He was glad to see Blayk pacing in the distance and knew he wouldn't have to harass any of the medical staff to find his mate.

"How is she?" Chris asked.

"Still no change. She hasn't regained consciousness yet, and they've just taken her to get an MRI scan and an X-ray."

"It's not good that she hasn't woken up yet, is it?"

"No. The longer she's out, the more likely it is that she's sustained brain damage. There is swelling in her brain, and even though she heals at a much more rapid pace, it may take longer for her body to repair itself, depending on how extensive the inflammation is," Blayk stated, a frown on his face.

"Fuck. If that bastard hadn't broken his neck in the fall, I would rip him apart," Chris snarled.

"Yeah, me, too. We've done all we can. Now it's up to Talia and God," Blayk said.

Chris turned as he heard wheels rolling on the floor. His fury boiled to the surface again at the sight of his mate looking so bruised and battered, hooked up to a drip as the staff wheeled her into a room close by. He felt so helpless. He wanted to take Talia into his arms and take her pain and bruises away, but he couldn't. He wanted to scream and shout at the unfairness of his woman being in such a state, but knew that wouldn't help her.

He walked over to Blayk as his brother conversed with the doctor and listened as he related Talia's injuries.

"She has bruises and contusions and is exhausted. She had a slight concussion but not enough to keep her out this long. I think you'll find she's just plain worn out. The cut on her chin has been stitched and bandaged as you can see. There is no swelling in her brain, and she will probably wake up once she's caught up on her sleep. We found traces of a drug in her system, so that could also be the cause of her sleeping. We'll keep an eye on her. Don't worry, she'll be fine."

"Thanks, doctor," Blayk said and shook the man's hand.

Chris stepped forward to do the same. "Thank you."

Chris watched the doctor walk away, and then he turned and entered the bedroom where Talia was convalescing. He pulled up a chair and sat by her side. He took her hand in his, careful not to touch the needle of the IV. The last thing he wanted was to cause her more pain.

"Talia, darlin'. You're safe now. It's time to wake up," Chris stated then looked over as James and Blayk pulled chairs up to the bed. James ran his hand up and down her blanket-covered shin, and Blayk took her other hand in his own.

"Please wake up, baby. We're getting worried about you," Blayk said.

"Come on, sugar. It's time to open those pretty eyes of yours," James declared.

Chris looked up at Talia's face when he felt her move her fingers in his hand. She licked her dry lips, and he knew in that instant that their woman was going to be fine. She moaned, and her eyelids fluttered, and then he was looking into her glazed deep-blue eyes.

"Hey, darlin', how are you feeling?" Chris asked.

"Terrible. Can I have some water please?"

"Sure, darlin'. Sorry, I should have thought about that," Chris said as he released her hand and got her a cup of water. He placed the flexible straw in the cup and held it to her lips. Talia took a few sips, then let her head fall back on the pillow.

"What happened?" Talia asked.

"Don't you remember, baby?" Blayk asked.

"Yes, I think so. Oh, I pushed Paul down the stairs, but I ended up falling with him. Any wonder I feel like I do. How did you find me?"

"We found the chip, darlin'," Chris answered.

"What chip?" Talia asked with a frown.

"Paul had placed an information chip in your license. We think it was his backup in case the people he was working with turned on him and stole his data. The chip had the address for all his properties as well as information on the mob and the experiments he had been doing with werewolf DNA," Chris explained.

"Oh my God. He was taking me down to his lab and he was going to use me as a lab rat. He said he was going to make me into his werewolf bitch. You have to stop him. The chaos he could create would be astronomical if he's allowed to get away with what he wants to do," Talia said urgently. She struggled to sit up, and Chris held her shoulders to keep her in place.

"Shh, it's okay now, darlin'. He won't be doing any experiments, and we destroyed his formula," Chris said in a quiet, soothing voice.

"He won't be hurting anyone ever again, baby. It's over," Blayk stated quietly.

"Did you call the police? Did they take him away? He's mentally unstable. He should be in a psychiatric hospital."

"Sugar, Paul's dead. He broke his neck when he fell down the stairs," James said quietly.

Talia went still, her face blank with shock. "He's dead? Oh my. I killed him?"

"Talia, you didn't kill him. Everything that happened to Paul was caused by his own actions. You had nothing to do with his death," Chris stated quietly.

"But…" Talia began.

"No buts, baby. You just concentrate on getting better, so we can get you home again. Okay?" Blayk declared.

"Okay," Talia replied around a yawn.

"Close your eyes, darlin'. You need to rest. We'll be here when you wake up," Chris said as he stood and placed a kiss on her forehead. Moments later Talia's breathing deepened and evened out. She was resting peacefully.

Chapter Nine

Talia shifted and felt their eyes on her. She looked up to see all her men watching her.

Three days had passed since the kidnapping, and Talia was back home. Her mates had been true to their word and stayed with her the whole time she had been in the hospital. They had taken turns staying with her through the night. She was never left alone at any given moment. She was currently lying in Chris's bed snuggled up between her mates. She had no lasting effects from her concussion, and the bruising on her cheek and chin were waning. She was glad Blayk was a doctor because that meant she didn't have to worry about going anywhere for a checkup. Her claiming had enhanced her healing abilities, and Blayk was going to take the stitches out of her chin today. She couldn't wait because they were driving her crazy with the itching. She didn't care if the incident left her with an unsightly scar. She was just glad to alive and the same person she had been before Paul had taken her.

"Morning, darlin', how do you feel?" Chris asked as he leaned over her.

"I'm fine, thanks, but I need to get up. I want a shower and food, and then I want to go work in the gardens."

"I don't think you should be doing anything yet, baby. You've only been home one night," Blayk stated.

"I feel fine, Blayk. I promise. If I get tired I'll stop. Please? I just need to get out in some fresh air."

"Okay, but only for a couple of hours," Blayk replied.

"Thank you. I promise not to overdo it. When or if I feel tired, I will come back inside to take a nap."

"Okay, let's get going then. I have to be at work in an hour," Blayk said, rising from the bed.

Talia rose and headed for the bathroom. Minutes later Blayk knocked on the door, and she opened it to him.

"Let me get those stitches out for you, baby. Then we'll help you in the shower."

Talia stood still with her neck tilted back while Blayk removed her stitches. She sighed and massaged the back of her neck as she lowered her head.

"Come on, darlin', I'll help you shower," Chris stated when he entered the bathroom.

"I can shower by myself, you know."

"I know you can, Talia. Humor me, okay? I like taking care of you. We all do," Chris explained.

Talia stepped into the shower with Chris. He washed her hair, and she was amused at how careful he was with her, trying not to get shampoo in her face. He washed her body thoroughly, being just as careful to touch every part of her, and by the time he was finished, she was so turned on she was shaking.

"Come here, darlin'. Let me take care of you," Chris said.

"You already have," Talia said with a sigh.

"Let me make you come, darlin'. I can smell and feel your need," Chris said in a deep voice as he pulled her into his arms.

Talia sighed again as her hard nipples came into contact with his bare stomach. The ache in her pussy intensified, and her internal muscles clenched. She was on fire, and she wanted him to make love to her. She clutched at his shoulders as he lifted her up. He placed a supporting arm beneath her butt and leaned down to kiss her.

Talia moaned as Chris's tongue swept into her mouth. She twined hers around his and clung to him. She felt his free hand slide in between their bodies, and his fingers began to massage her clit. She sobbed with need as she sucked on his lower lip, and then she cried out when she felt him plunge two fingers into her wet cunt. He pumped his digits in and out of her body, hooking them as he reached just inside the entrance to her pussy.

Talia threw her head back and moaned as waves of pleasure cascaded through her. She felt Chris move his thumb into the top of her slit, and he caressed her clit as he fucked her with his fingers. She keened in the back of her throat as the tight coils in her womb and pussy gathered and then snapped. She screamed as her body convulsed, contractions washing over her in wave after wave of ecstasy. Chris didn't stop pumping his fingers into her until the last spasm faded away.

"You are so fucking sexy. I love watching you come, darlin'," he said in a deep, rumbling voice which caused her to shiver. "Come on, I have work to do."

Chris turned the shower off and passed her over to Blayk, who was waiting with a large towel. He patted her dry and toweled her hair. James was at the ready with the hair dryer, and she stood still while he brushed her tresses. She had never felt so loved and cherished. She wanted to bask in their attention forever. She opened her eyes, reached for his hand, and kissed his palm.

"Thank you," Talia said, looking into James's eyes.

"You're welcome, sugar. Why don't you go and get dressed? I'm going to shower and I'll meet you downstairs for breakfast," James suggested.

"Okay," Talia replied and left the bathroom. She dressed in her favorite jeans and one of the new tops she had bought and then headed downstairs with Chris at her side.

The large dining room was nearly filled to capacity. Instead of sitting down at the table, she helped the housekeeper and cook, Angie, and her daughter, Cindy, by taking platters of food to the massive dining table. She took a seat when that was done and waited for Blayk and James before she ate breakfast. They walked through the door a moment later. Her breath caught in her throat as she watched her sexy mates walking toward her. She knew in that instant she was irrevocably in love with her three men. They took such good care of her, and they had wrangled their way into her heart. Talia had vowed, after Paul, she was never going to be involved with another man. Boy, had she been wrong. Here she was mated to three hot, hunky men, and she never wanted to be apart from them. She smiled as love and joy filled her heart. Her mates filled and completed her as no one else ever could.

"Here, darlin', let me get you some breakfast," Chris whispered from her side. She turned to him and gave him a smile, letting him know how grateful she was for taking such good care of her.

Talia ate her breakfast and sipped her coffee when she was done. The room was so full of chattering people it was hard for her to stay tuned to any one conversation, so she gave up and just watched them all interact. She watched how Jonah, Mikhail, and Brock took care of their mate and then slid her eyes over to see Keira's mates taking care of her. She was so glad she hadn't been Paul's true mate. He and the Rogan Pack couldn't even compare to the men of the Friess Pack. They were all loyal to their Alphas and were so solicitous and took such good care of their women. She hadn't ever seen human males treat their women with such love and respect. She wanted to hold on to them and never let go.

When breakfast was over, Talia wandered out into the gardens. She loved watching plants grow and nurturing them until they rewarded her for her care with their colorful, fragrant blooms. Talia was weeding the vegetable garden when she heard footsteps nearby. Security had been beefed up since her kidnapping, and all the women were watched constantly. If their mates couldn't be near them, then one of the Omegas was appointed as bodyguard for the women. Everyone in the mansion always knew they could find Talia working in the gardens, and she was interrupted often as they sought her out. She looked up, and saw Michelle coming toward her.

"Hi," Talia called.

"Hi, yourself. How are you feeling?" Michelle asked.

"I'm okay."

"Are you happy here, Talia?" Michelle asked when she stopped in front of her.

"Yes. I've never been happier."

"The men take good care of us, don't they?"

"Yeah. I've never seen anything like that before. They are all so dominant, but they treat us women like we are precious."

"To them we are. The men only get one mate in a lifetime, and if they don't meet their mate, well, I'm sure you understand," Michelle stated. "Well, I'd better go check on the baby. Just remember you don't have to do that."

"I know, but I enjoy it. Thanks, Michelle," Talia said then got back to work.

Talia spent four hours in the garden. Time had gotten away from her, and when she looked at her watch and realized it was nearly lunchtime, she decided to call it a day. She went back inside, jumped into the shower, and cleaned up. By the time she was dry she was beginning to flag. The thought of crawling into Chris's bed, to have his and his brothers' scent surrounding her, was too good to miss. She pulled the towel from around her body, dropped it on the floor, and slid in between the sheets. She was sound asleep moments later.

Talia didn't want to wake up from her erotic dream. She spread her legs wide as fingers slid through the wet folds of her pussy. She moaned when a mouth latched on to one of her nipples while fingers pinched the other. She opened her mouth and sucked on the tongue which was thrust into her moist depths and slid her lips over the ones covering hers. She slowly came back to consciousness and realized she wasn't dreaming at all. She opened her eyes and looked in Chris's as he kissed her. Blayk was sucking and pinching on her nipples, and James was between her legs eating her cunt. She sucked in a breath as Chris moved his mouth from hers.

"Hey, darlin', did you enjoy your nap? Do you feel all right?"

"Yes," Talia cried out in answer to Chris, and also in response to the pleasure bestowed on her by James and Blayk.

"Do you want us, sugar?" James asked when he lifted his head to look at her.

"Yes. Please, now," Talia whimpered in need.

"We'll give you what you want, baby. Just let us love on you," Blayk said in a deep voice, and then she watched him lower his head to her breast again.

Talia mewled when James sucked and laved on her clit and pushed two fingers into her cunt. She reached up and threaded her fingers into Chris's hair. She pulled his mouth down to her and kissed him with all the emotions she felt for him. The heat and carnality of the kiss set her on fire, but it was also full of emotion. She felt tears prick the backs of her eyelids and tried to push them back. But her feelings were just too strong to contain, and tears leaked out from beneath her lids and down over her cheeks. The hands and mouths on her body pulled away instantly. Talia opened her eyes as she felt large, muscular arms scoop her up, and she found herself sitting on Chris's lap.

"Did we hurt you, Talia? Why are you crying?" Chris asked.

"No, you didn't hurt me. I'm just…I can't explain," Talia said haltingly.

"Darlin', we're worried about you. Please, tell me what's wrong," Chris said gently.

"Nothing's wrong. That's the problem," Talia said with a hitch in her voice.

"What do you mean, baby?" Blayk asked.

"Everything is just so right. And I felt so full of happiness and you guys treat me so well, I just couldn't contain my emotions," Talia said and ducked her head to hide her heated cheeks.

"You have nothing to be embarrassed about, sugar. We love you," James said and reached over to kiss her shoulder.

"You do?"

"Darlin', how could you doubt how we feel? You mean everything to us. I love you, Talia," Chris said, his voice full of emotion.

"I love you, too, baby," Blayk said and kissed her temple.

"Oh God," Talia cried as tears poured out of her eyes. "I love you, too. I love all of you so much, it hurts." Talia gave in to her emotions and let Chris hold her while she cried with joy. Her heart was so full that she had to release some of her feelings. When her tears finally slowed and dried, she looked up and gave her mates a chagrined smile.

"Do you feel better, baby?" Blayk asked her.

"Yes. I'm sorry for getting all sappy," she apologized.

"Don't you dare apologize for the way you feel, darlin'. We wanted to tell you we loved you the moment we set eyes on you, but we didn't want to scare you away. Now, as much as I want to continue what we started, we are going to be late for dinner if we don't haul ass. Tonight is a full moon and all the *weres* go for a run after dinner. When we get back we'll take up where we left off. Okay?" Chris asked.

"Okay," Talia replied. She was excited about tonight. She hadn't seen her men in their wolf forms yet. She was eager to see the color of their fur, and she wanted to run her fingers through it and scratch behind their ears. Talia grinned even more broadly. Seeing their wolves sounded almost as good as taking up where she had left off with them as men.

Chapter Ten

Talia had never seen such a festive atmosphere or so much food. It was a wonder the table wasn't bowing under the weight of the food platters. Jonah, along with his brothers, Mikhail and Brock, stood at the far end of the table. Michelle sat between Jonah and Mikhail.

"I would like you all to welcome the newest member to our pack. She has already won the heart of your queen and her friend. Welcome, Talia Black," Jonah said and raised a glass in her direction.

Talia acknowledged the Alphas and their mate with a nod of her head and then lowered her eyes. She had never expected to be welcomed into the pack so formally. The Friess Pack was just so different from what she had experienced with the Rogan Pack and her ex. She didn't really know what to do. She was thankful when all eyes were off of her and she could relax once more. She sat between Chris and Blayk and huffed with exasperation as they loaded her plate with food. She knew werewolves had a higher metabolism than humans, but why they kept loading her plate with so much was beyond her.

Dinner was a joyful, exuberant affair. There seemed to be an excited hum in the air which was contagious. When the meal was over and the *weres* began filing outside, Talia followed behind. She was eager to see her men as wolves. The thought that they could change form and were so much stronger than her, excited her. She made sure to keep out of the way and watched with awe as her men stripped off their clothes. Their bodies began to contort as their muscles shifted and reshaped. The popping and cracking sounded painful, but once they were in their wolf forms, their joyful howls sent shivers racing up and down her spine.

Talia took a hesitant step forward and then stopped. Her mates turned toward her and walked slowly to her side. She could tell by the color of their eyes and their coats who was who. Plus, Chris was more muscular and taller than Blayk and James. He nudged her hand with his nose, and she laughed. She lifted her hand and scratched behind his ears and then ran her fingers through his soft, glossy coat. She did the same to Blayk and James. They each licked her on the hand and then turned, running into the woods at the back of the house. She had never seen such a beautiful sight.

Talia trudged back toward the house. She knew her mates could be gone all night. Her ex had often disappeared for days on end. She reached the house and walked to the living room. She found Michelle sitting with her baby as she fed him.

"Where's Keira?" Talia asked as she sat down.

"She's gone for a run. I'm surprised you didn't see her out there," Michelle replied.

"How did Keira become a werewolf?" Talia asked curiously.

"Poor Keira didn't really get a say in the matter. It was either change her and hope she survived, or she would have died anyway. She'd been shot, and she was dying," Michelle said, and looked at her with sadness in her eyes.

"How does one get changed into a werewolf?"

"Are you sure you want to know? It's pretty horrific."

"I'd really like to know. I always thought a werewolf had to be born with the gene," Talia said.

"Well, you're right, but a human can be changed. Whether they survive the process or not is another matter. She had to be savaged by a werewolf so the wolf DNA could get into her system. It was touch and go for a while, but she pulled through and now she is happy with her mates and carrying a child."

"Oh my God. That's horrible. The thought of her mates having to hurt her is just too horrendous to even think about," Talia said, covering her mouth.

"Her mates didn't do it. They couldn't bear the thought of hurting her. My mates and some of the other pack members held her mates back while Chris changed her and then Blayk took over caring for her," Michelle clarified. "I hope no one ever has to do that again. It made me sick to my stomach. I was just glad Keira was already unconscious. The thought of her going through that, having to endure such agony is beyond my comprehension."

"Oh wow. Chris did it? I just can't imagine... He's always so gentle. It must have caused him terrible anguish to have to do that," Talia said quietly.

"It did. He was on tenterhooks the whole time Keira was recovering. Even though he knew Keira would have died without him changing her, he would have felt guilty if she had died afterward," Michelle said.

Talia looked up to see tears in Michelle's eyes. She gave her a watery smile, and they both laughed with joy when baby Stefan let out a great belch, easing the tension of the moment.

"He's so cute. He looks like Jonah," Talia said as she stroked a finger down his baby-soft cheek. He smiled, but his eyes were closed and Talia knew he was already falling asleep. She pictured herself round with child, and then she saw herself holding her own baby in her arms with her mates surrounding her. She felt a deep tug and yearning and knew that she wanted to be the mother of their babies, just as much as she wanted to be their mate.

"Let me go and put him down, and then I'll be back so we can chat," Michelle said as she stood and walked from the room.

Talia smiled as the sweet baby smell left the room. She wondered if her mates would be averse to starting to try for a baby right away. She was on the pill, but she knew she wanted to have her babies early, and the practice of making love regularly was definitely something to look forward to. She looked up when she heard footsteps coming from the entryway. She smiled at Cindy as she hurried into the kitchen. The young woman's cheeks were flushed, and Talia could tell she had been out for a run. She wondered what it was like. To be able to change forms and run free through the woods would be such a joy.

Talia jumped when she heard a loud crash emanate from the kitchen. She got to her feet and froze in the doorway when she heard another thud and crash. The hair on her nape stood up on end, and she had a bad feeling in her gut. She got to the door of the living room and halted. A large, strange man came into view. She took a step into the hall and backed away, but he followed. She saw a flash of silver as he moved toward her, and she looked down. He held a knife in his hand. She didn't know who he was or what he wanted, but from the looks of it, nothing good would come out of this.

Talia felt her heel connect with the stairs. She lifted her foot and began to slowly walk up the stairs, backward. She kept her eyes on his, too afraid to look away in case he came at her with the knife.

"Who are you? What do you want?" Talia asked.

"I'm looking for Talia Rogan."

Talia froze. Anyone who called her by that name had to be associated with Paul—as if the knife wasn't bad enough.

"She's not here," she replied, hoping Michelle wouldn't choose that moment to return. Her foremost thought, even as she looked at the knife pointing toward her, was that Michelle and her baby needed to stay safe. "What do you want with her anyway?"

"She has something that belonged to her dearly departed husband. A little information that he was stupid enough to leave with her. I want it!"

"Who are you?" Talia asked and blanched as he gave her a smile so full of evil, she felt sick to her stomach.

"Tony Picotti," he said.

Talia felt all the blood drain from her face as he introduced himself. He looked proud of who he was. She felt her stomach twist again.

"I see you've heard of me. I'm glad to know my reputation precedes me," he said and placed a foot on the bottom step.

Talia cringed inside with fear. She couldn't believe the leader of the biggest drug cartel in the United States of America was standing in front of her. She remembered Paul telling her he had a hold over the mob, but it seemed the drug lord had decided he was going to be leader of all the *weres*. *Why does this shit keep happening to me? Why do I seem to draw the sickos to my side? Oh God, please help me keep Michelle and baby Stefan safe!*

Talia made it to the first-floor landing. She wanted to turn and run, but she knew Michelle's suite of rooms was on this level, and the last thing she wanted was to lead the evil bastard to his goals. She ignored the landing and began to move up the steps faster, hoping she wouldn't misplace her feet as she was moving backward. She heard footsteps and knew her luck had run out. She turned her head and saw Michelle walking along the first-floor hallway.

She pleaded with her eyes for Michelle to run. Talia sighed with relief as Michelle fled back down the corridor and turned to flee when Tony Picotti was distracted by the sight of the bolting woman. She didn't get very far. She screamed in pain as a tight fist gripped her hair, and she fell back a couple of steps, slamming into the chest of the evil man behind her.

Talia froze when she felt the cold steel of the knife blade against her throat..

"Tell me," Tony snarled in her ear, "was that Talia? Maybe I need to go introduce myself to her."

"No," she whimpered. "I'm Talia. I'm the one you're looking for." She was so scared that her whole body was cold and she was trembling uncontrollably. But if she could keep the man from going after Michelle, at least her Alpha queen and baby Stefan would be safe. Deciding she may as well finish the job, she blurted, "That chip you're looking for is gone! My mates destroyed it. There's no more werewolf serum." Some part of her had hoped he would let her go once he knew the truth, but Tony only gripped her more tightly.

"I don't believe you," he said in her ear. "Did your useless husband give you the serum already? I know he wanted to make you his queen." He paused, his breath hot in Talia's ear. "Maybe he had the right idea."

"I am not a werewolf, and I wouldn't fuck you if you were the last man on Earth," Talia raged then ground the heel of her shoe against his shin.

Talia sobbed when he just cursed and didn't let her go. He pulled on her hair so hard, tears of pain leaked from her eyes.

Low rumbling growls and howls filled the air, and she knew in that moment her mates and the other males of the pack were close by.

"You won't get away with this. You're surrounded by werewolves. They will rip you apart," Talia said and cursed the wobble she heard in her own voice.

"Nah. You are my ticket out of here, sweetness. God, you smell nice. I can't wait to fuck you," Tony whispered in her ear. "You're coming with me. I can use you to bargain for that serum."

Talia gagged. She was surrounded by his evil stench and was afraid she would be sick. He wrapped an arm tightly around her breasts and shoulders and began to pull her down the stairs. The tip of the knife blade had pierced her skin in several places on her throat, the cuts were stinging, and she could feel her blood trickling down over her neck.

Tony pulled her toward the side door which led to the carport outside. She didn't know if her mates and the other wolves would be able to save her. Tony held the knife tight across her throat. She was too scared to swallow in case she ended up hurting herself against the sharp blade. He walked her through the open doorway and pulled her out into the night.

The hair on her nape stood on end as growls erupted all around them. Tony didn't stop. He just kept right on going. They were surrounded by wolves, but that didn't seem to faze Picotti. Her eyes connected with Chris's, Blayk's, and James's. She let them see all the love she felt for them in her eyes. She could see their fury as they looked back at her, but she could also see their anguish. She didn't want to leave the loves of her life. She had only just found them. Tony didn't give any of the wolves a chance to get at him from behind. He kept his back to the wall of the carport, and then pulled her through the open door of the large SUV.

Talia hoped for an opportunity to escape, but she didn't get the chance. He got into the front of the vehicle and pulled her on top of him.

"Close the door or I'll slit your throat here and now," Tony commanded harshly.

Talia reached for the door and pulled it closed, the sound of the locks engaging echoing through the car. There was an awkward scuffle as Tony tried to get across the front seat. She whimpered as he pushed her off his lap and into the driver's seat and handed her the keys.

"Drive, bitch."

It took Talia three tries before she was able to get the key in the ignition. She gave her mates one last look and drove down the driveway. Talia knew she was never going to see her mates again.

Chapter Eleven

Chris memorized the license plate as he watched his mate disappear from sight. He changed back to his human form and raced for the study. He stopped short when the smell of blood permeated his senses. He looked behind him to see Blayk and James, as well as his Alphas and the others, on his heels. Blayk sniffed, taking in the coppery smell of blood, and then his brother headed for the kitchen. Someone in there was hurt or even dead. He couldn't think about that now. He wanted to get to the phone and report Talia's abduction to the authorities. The sooner there was an APB out on the vehicle and the asshole that had his mate, the better.

Men went running in every direction. His Alphas bounded up the stairs, obviously intent on checking on their mate and son. Chris ran toward the study. He grabbed the phone and dialed 9-1-1. James entered the room and threw some clothes at him as he hung up the phone. He pulled them on and grabbed his keys. Blayk would be busy tending to whoever was hurt, so it was up to him and James to track Talia. He ran outside and got into his truck. James was close behind him, and his brother jumped in his own vehicle. They went roaring down the driveway, heedless of the gravel spraying from beneath their tires.

Chris turned right at the end of the drive, and James headed left. They had to split up if they wanted to find their mate. Chris's heart beat a painful, rapid tattoo in his chest. He felt sick to his stomach with fear as he remembered the blood trickling down Talia's throat from several nicks in her skin. He wanted to find that motherfucker and tear his head from his body. Chris knew who the fucker was on sight. He had found his name when he looked at Paul's Swiss bank account. He had run a check on Tony Picotti and had found a photograph of the bastard in a large newspaper.

He pushed the *answer* button on his Bluetooth when his cell phone rang.

"Yeah," Chris snapped.

"Hey, man, we're on our way to help." Greg's voice came over the speaker. "You need to be very careful if you find them. The man who has her is the mob leader, Tony Picotti."

"I know. Fuck," Chris roared, fear forming a larger knot in his gut. "He's won't hesitate to kill my mate. We have to find them."

"The cops are on it and the Feds have been called in. If we can't find him, they will," Greg stated. "I'll be on your tail in a few."

"Does James know who we're dealing with?" Chris asked.

"Yeah, Jake's calling him as we speak. Cindy was hurt, but Blayk's looking after her and she'll be fine in a couple of days."

"What about Michelle and Stefan?"

"Safe and well. Your woman let Michelle know there was danger and she locked herself in her rooms."

"Thank God."

"Yeah. The Feds are already in Aztec. They had a tail on Picotti, but he gave them the slip. They're scouring the countryside for him. He won't get away," Greg said.

"That's not what I'm worried about. He has my woman and she's hurt. God, I can still see the blood on her throat," Chris rumbled.

"Keep it together, man. You can't lose it now. Talia needs you," Greg said in a calm voice.

"Yeah, I know," Chris replied with a sigh.

"I'm on your six," Greg stated.

"I see you. Thanks, Greg," Chris said and ended the call.

* * * *

Talia was so scared, she was in danger of wetting her pants. She was having trouble concentrating on driving. The SUV swerved again, and she corrected the wheel as she felt the knife blade prick the skin of her neck, yet again.

"Keep it together, bitch. You and me are gonna have so much fun. I can just see it now. I am going to have all the werewolves bowing down to me and nobody is going to be able to stop me."

Her peripheral vision caught movement, and Talia glanced over at him. He grabbed hold of her hair and ran his tongue up the side of her face, and then he laughed at her as she tried to shrink away. Her stomach roiled with revulsion. Air rushed in and out of her mouth as she tried to control her nausea. She had no idea where they were going, but she tried to push her panic down deep. She had to try and keep her wits about her if she was going to have a chance at escaping the sick bastard.

She tried to reason with him. "I told you that I don't have the information you're looking for. Now you've got a lot of angry wolves after you."

"Yeah," Tony grunted. He didn't sound nearly as confident as he had before. "Those wolves…Big, aren't they?"

She could tell he was rattled. It crossed Talia's mind that he'd panicked back on the stairs when he heard the wolves returning. Probably he had never intended on kidnapping her in the first place. The thought filled her with helpless rage. Why did this keep happening to her? Why was it she always ended up in trouble and in the hands of sick motherfuckers? Maybe she could grab the upper hand now that Picotti was nervous. She took a few deep breaths and pushed her fear to the back of her consciousness.

Talia saw flashing blue-and-red lights up ahead and knew the police were looking for her. Her men must have contacted the authorities, and she felt relief permeate her body when she finally realized she wasn't alone. She hoped Chris, Blayk, and James were okay. She knew they would be out looking for her. She had seen the anguish in their eyes even when they were still in their wolf forms. She had wanted to run to them and hug them to her tight.

Talia slowed the SUV as the flashing lights came closer and closer. She hoped the police would be able to cut her off and get her out of Tony's clutches. The man had such insane dreams of power and grandeur. She only wished the prick hadn't pulled his safety belt on.

"Put your foot flat to the floor and don't swerve," Tony commanded in a hard voice.

"What? Are you trying to get us killed?" Talia asked incredulously.

"Don't sweat it, sweetheart. Cops don't play chicken very well," he replied with a chuckle, then pricked her neck with the knife. "Do it!"

Talia was thankful they were on a straight stretch of road and prayed she would be able to keep the vehicle under control. She planted her foot on the accelerator, and the pedal met the floor. She clutched the wheel so hard her knuckles turned white.

The police flew past the car, a blur on either side of her since she was now driving in the middle of the road. She glanced in the rearview mirror and saw smoke rising from the tires as they slid along the asphalt of the road.

She looked out front again and saw more lights up ahead. It didn't look like they were moving. She just hoped they hadn't blocked the entire road. The last thing she wanted to do was crash into a stationary vehicle at such a high speed. She glanced down to the dash and gasped when she saw how fast they were traveling. She knew that if she were to crash she would be a dead woman.

A bubble of hysteria rose in her throat in the form of laughter. She didn't know what she was worrying for. She was a dead woman anyway. There was no way in hell she was letting that bastard touch her. *Think, Talia. You have to do something! You can't let him win!*

Talia sped past the two police cars on the side of the road. She heard a pop, and then she struggled with the steering wheel. The police must have put spikes across the road, and now the tires of the vehicle had blown out. She slammed on the brakes and used all her strength to keep the vehicle straight and upright. She felt the car teeter on two wheels, and she pulled her foot from the brake. The SUV slammed back down onto four wheels, and she went to put her foot on the brake, but the knife at her throat pressed harder.

"Floor it, sweet cheeks."

"What? Are you out of your mind? We have no tires," Talia cried.

"Do as you're told. Floor it now!"

Talia slammed her foot onto the accelerator, and the screech the rims made against the asphalt set her teeth on edge. They weren't traveling nearly as fast now, and she wondered how Tony thought he could escape.

"Pull into the roadside stop, twenty yards ahead."

Talia did as she was told and pulled the vehicle up and into the rest stop.

"Come on, sweetheart. We're going for a little walk," Tony said and pulled her across the seat and out the door.

Talia cried out with pain as he pulled her by the hair and her thigh scraped on the door of the car. A sharp piece of metal cut into her thigh. She stumbled, trying to get her feet beneath her, and then he was pulling her in amongst the trees. Shit, the police were never going to be able to find them out here. It was dark, but the moon's glow made it easier for her to see. Tony would have the advantage over the law. He could hide them amongst the shadows and watch as the police searched for them. She stumbled over a tree root and would have fallen if Tony hadn't been gripping her hair so tightly. And then her brain began to kick into gear.

She was going to escape. Come hell or high water, she was getting out of his clutches. She watched the ground carefully, looking for the perfect place to stage her plan. She pushed her fear down deep and thought through all the possible scenarios. They all led to her death. She didn't have a choice. If she was going to get out of this, she would have to take a risk.

She saw the large tree root and the rocks strewn around it. She had found the perfect location.

Talia made sure to hook her toe beneath the root and used her body weight to push herself forward so she fell to the ground. She cried out as the palm of her hand connected with a sharp rock, slicing her skin. The hold he had on her hair hurt her scalp, but he let her go so he wouldn't go tumbling to the ground with her. She didn't care about the pain. She pushed it to the back of her mind. Pain let her know she was still alive.

"Get up, bitch," Tony barked out.

Talia pushed up from the ground, her hand closing around the rock, and she stumbled again. He must have put the knife away, because she felt two hands on her shoulders helping her to her feet. She tensed her muscles and swung up with all her might. The rock connected with the side of Tony's head, and he let her go. Talia took off.

She ran and ran and ran. Her lungs burned from lack of oxygen, her head and neck throbbed, and her thigh ached, but she didn't stop. She was so scared she couldn't see straight. She had no idea in which direction she was heading, but she didn't care. As long as it was away from him. She heard a loud roar, and she knew he was after her.

Talia ran faster. She was heedless of the branches slapping against her face and body. She darted around trees, jumped over fallen tree trunks, and stumbled over rocks. She could hear water, and if she could find it, she might find somewhere to hole up, like a cave or hollow. The sound of the water would cover any sounds she made. She saw the dead log at the last minute. She jumped over it and then opened her mouth on a silent scream. She was falling.

Her stomach rose up into her throat, and she looked down. She saw some sort of tree limb at the last minute and reached out. One of her hands caught hold, and her arm was nearly pulled from its socket as the limb halted her fall. She looked down and whimpered with fear and closed her eyes. She was hanging by a thick tree root on the side of a cliff wall.

She reached up with her other hand, and the bark on the tree limb bit into her sliced palm. It hurt badly, but she just gripped tighter. She was hanging at least twenty yards from the ground, and she had nowhere to go. She looked up, and even though she might have been able to climb back to the top, she was too scared to. Tony was looking for her.

Talia used every bit of strength she possessed and tried to pull herself up onto the thick root. Her arms shook, and she wouldn't be able to hold on much longer. She couldn't pull herself up, but maybe if she could hook her legs up over the limb she would be more secure. She began to swing slightly, forward and back, gaining momentum as she did. She flipped her body through her arms, and the backs of her calves slammed down over the root. She slid her thighs back a little until her knees were hooked over the limb. She was just in time. The strength in her arms gave out, and she ended up hanging upside down over the drop. Her arms felt like lead weights hanging above her head. Her whole body trembled with shock, cold, and fear. She couldn't hang upside down for long, but at least she was giving her arms a rest for the moment.

Tears leaked from her eyes, and her right shoulder was aching so badly now that she wasn't using her arms. Talia heard movement above her and lifted her head. She thought she saw a glint of light, but she wasn't certain. She breathed lightly and shallowly as she listened. The sound of cussing reached her ears, and it faded as Tony Picotti moved away.

Talia wanted to sag with relief, but she was still in danger. She wouldn't feel safe until she was back in the arms of her men. She turned and lifted her head toward the cliff wall, trying to find something to hold on to so she could pull herself upright. Her head pounded from all the adrenaline she had running through her system, and hanging upside down definitely did not help. She saw another smaller tree root sticking out from the rock wall, but she couldn't reach it just yet.

Talia swung up, and her hands gripped the rough bark. She began to inch her way closer to the wall. It was torture on her sore shoulder and hand and a painstakingly slow process, but she was making headway. She was finally within reach of the other small limb and had just stretched out for it when she heard a crack. She whimpered as the limb she was on jolted.

Chapter Twelve

Chris saw police cars driving toward him. As they came into view, they hooked and did a one-eighty, accelerating in the direction Chris himself was driving. Smoke poured out from beneath the tires as they slid over the tarmac. He pushed his foot flat to the floor and sped along behind the cops. He and the cars in front of him sped past two stationary cop cars, and he saw one of the officers pick up the spike from the side of the road. He knew that the vehicle Talia had been in was now incapacitated. "Thank you, God," he muttered.

Chris followed the police into a rest stop off the side of the road and slid to a stop. The officers were out of their cars and had their weapons trained on him in moments.

"Put your hands up, now," one of the officers yelled.

Chris sighed and raised his hands. He didn't want to have to deal with this shit, but he knew he would have done the same thing if he were in their shoes. He just wanted to find his mate.

His door was opened, and he was pulled from his truck. He didn't offer any resistance as the officer cuffed him and pushed him into the side of his vehicle. The cop searched his pockets and pulled out his wallet.

"What are you doing here, Mr. Friess?" the officer asked.

"I am looking for my wife. That asshole Tony Picotti has her," Chris growled out.

"Let him go, Smith," another voice said from behind him.

"Yes, sir," Smith answered.

Chris felt the cuffs fall away, and then he turned around slowly, not wanting to startle the young Officer Smith.

"I'm Sergeant Royce Waverly, this is Officer Colin Smith. I'm sorry for the confusion, Mr. Friess, but I'm sure you understand the caution," Waverly explained.

"Yes, don't worry about it. Where are they?" Chris asked as he surreptitiously sniffed the air.

"Picotti's taken her into the woods. Backup will be here any moment. I think you should go home and wait for us to do our job," Waverly suggested.

"How would you feel if it was your wife or girlfriend? I'm staying and there's nothing you can do about it," Chris stated adamantly.

"Just stay out of the way," Waverly ordered with steel in his voice and tried to glare Chris down.

Chris pretended to back off as he looked down and replied, "Yes, sir."

He watched as Waverly and Smith disappeared amongst the trees. He heard another car coming and knew the backup had arrived. The officers got out of their car and didn't even spare him a glance. Chris reached for his cell phone and dialed James. He let his brother know what was happening and where they were so he could spread the word, then ended the call.

Chris's ears pricked up when he heard another vehicle coming. He looked up and sighed with relief when he spotted Greg's truck. *His* backup had just arrived.

"Where are they?" Greg asked, and sniffed the air. He didn't have to answer, because Greg's wolf would have picked up and sorted through all the scents in the air. "There are a lot of cliffs and ravines around here. You change forms and I'll follow with a rope just in case."

Chris nodded to Greg and stripped out of his clothes. He looked around and inhaled, making sure it was safe for him to change without being seen, then called his wolf forth. He took off into the trees, Greg running behind him.

He sniffed the ground and air, his nose leading the way. A growl rumbled up out of his mouth when he smelled Talia's blood and that of Tony Picotti. When he saw that their tracks led in two different directions, he knew Talia had managed to escape the bastard for a while, and he took off again, following Talia's scent.

He wondered where the cops were looking. He hadn't sighted them since he had entered the woods. Wherever they were, they were looking in the wrong direction. He sniffed again and caught their scent. They had followed Picotti's trail. He gave a soft yip and took off running again. He nearly fell to his haunches when Talia's scent stopped on the edge of a ravine. He threw back his head and let out a mournful howl as grief pierced his heart.

"Wait. Be quiet, Chris," Greg said as he came to stand at his side.

Chris clamped his jaws tight, stopping his noise of grief. And then he heard her. The sound of her voice was faint. He didn't know if she was afraid or hurt or both, but she was alive. He stepped up closer to the cliff edge, and using his enhanced wolf vision, he looked over the side.

His heart stopped beating for a moment and then slammed against his chest. She was hanging from a tree root, and the limb looked like it was about to break. He pushed his wolf back and changed into his human form.

"I'm here, darlin'. Hang on, we'll get you. Don't you dare let go," Chris commanded. He turned to see Greg was already securing the rope he carried around the trunk of a large tree close to the edge. He only hoped the rope would be long enough. He wanted to go down there and help Talia, but he knew that root could go at any time. He grabbed the now-secured rope and threw it over the side. He lay down on his stomach, heedless of branches and stones digging into his naked skin and swung the rope over until it was within Talia's reach.

"Talia," Chris called out, "you need to get that rope secured around you so we can pull you up, darlin'."

"Okay," Talia replied. Chris could tell by the wobble in her voice she was tired and scared. He wanted to be able to reach over and pluck her up into his arms. He was scared the limb would break before they could get her up.

He watched as Talia reached out for the rope. He swung it over a bit more, and Talia was going to have to get on top of the limb to have enough to length to wrap around her waist and tie it off.

"It's too short, Chris," Talia sobbed.

"You have to get up on top of that root, darlin'. It's the only way. Come on. You can do it, Talia. Just move nice and slow and pull yourself up. Good girl." Chris spoke calmly, but his insides were full of terror.

He held his breath as he watched his mate struggle. He could see her arms and legs quivering with fatigue as she tried to pull herself up. She reached out and grabbed hold of a skinny twig with the last of her ebbing strength and pulled herself on the topside of the limb. She was practically lying along the length. Talia slowly eased herself into an upright sitting position, her legs straddling the root. He shifted the rope until it was within her reach, and he held it still as she wrapped it beneath her arms and above her breasts. She wrapped the bound end in and out of the loop around her then tied it off. He prayed to God the knot would hold.

"Okay, she's secure," Chris turned and told Greg.

"Chris," Talia screamed. He grabbed hold of the rope and held tight just as the root broke and fell. The rope pulled taut, and he held on as Talia swung and hit the cliff wall. Her cry of pain pierced his heart, but he had her secure. He began to pull on the rope hand over hand, with excruciating slowness. Greg was at his side when the top of Talia's head came into view, and then Greg held the rope steady. Chris pulled her up and laid her on the ground.

She had a bruise and cut on her forehead from where she had hit the rocks of the cliff wall, and blood trickled over her face. She had nicks and cuts on her neck where that bastard had cut her, and her palm was sliced open, blood covering her arm. But she was conscious and alive. Greg pulled the rope from around her, and then Chris lifted her into his arms.

Chris was shaking like a leaf, just as Talia was, and she clutched the hair between his pecs and bawled into his chest. He rubbed his hands up and down her back, trying to offer comfort as he came to terms with how close he was to losing his mate, forever.

Chris looked up to find Greg standing behind the tree trunk. He loosened the rope from the tree, and then Chris turned his head as a loud snap echoed close by. Tony Picotti came striding out of the trees, knife raised and pointing at him and Talia. The bastard hadn't seen Greg. He saw more movement down the path and sighted James and Blayk heading toward them.

"I thought she was dead. Thank you for finding my bitch for me. Let her go and move away," Picotti commanded.

Chris heard Talia whimper, and then he gently placed her on the ground at his side. He stood slowly, not wanting to alarm the motherfucker standing before him.

"The woods are crawling with cops and the Feds by now. You won't get away with this," Chris stated quietly as he moved in front of Talia. "She doesn't have anything you want, anyway."

"That's what you think. I've got the law walking around in circles. They'll be at it for hours before they figure out where I am. And by then we'll be long gone," Picotti snarled. "She may not have what I want, but you and your werewolf pals do. I'm sure you'll give it to me in exchange for her."

Chris inched his way toward Picotti, placing more and more distance between him and his woman. He lowered his head and surreptitiously looked for Greg. His cousin was ready to help out, but it looked like his brothers were going to take the bastard out. His brothers were creeping up behind Picotti in wolf form, and the prick was totally oblivious. Chris kicked a stone toward Picotti, trying to distract him.

"That won't work, you know. I'm going to kill you right where you stand," Picotti stated and readied the knife.

"No, you won't. They'll kill you first," Chris replied.

Tony Picotti spun round and screamed in terror as a big wolf with light-brown fur leapt at him. He didn't even get to use the knife. James's vicious sharp teeth ripped out his throat, and he was dead before he hit the ground.

Chris caught the clothes he had stripped off previously as Greg threw them at him and he hastily re-dressed. He picked Talia up in his arms, cradling her tightly against his chest as he walked back toward the parking area. Blayk and James were just getting their clothes out of their trucks when his Alphas and other pack members arrived. He sat down on the tailgate of his truck, Talia on his lap and in his arms, while Blayk tended to their mate. Chris was not willing to relinquish his hold on her.

Greg had found the police and Feds and showed them where Picotti's body was, and he was now back, with the rest of them. Chris looked over at Greg and nodded his head in thanks to his cousin.

The police and the Feds took their statements and then organized for the coroner to take Picotti's body away. Of course, he, Talia, and Greg had told the law that the wolf that had attacked the drug lord had disappeared into the night. They were relieved that the police didn't question them further.

"I'll stitch your hand up when we get back home, sugar. It's clean and wrapped, which is all I can to for now. Okay?" Blayk asked.

Talia nodded her head, and then she leaned against Chris and closed her eyes. She was sound asleep moments later. He handed the keys to his truck over to Greg's brother Jake and climbed into the backseat with his mate. He held her tightly to his body the whole way home.

Chapter Thirteen

Talia smiled when she heard the bedroom door slam against the opposite wall. It was showtime.

She couldn't wait to put her plan into action. She was so full of excitement that she was having trouble containing her emotions. But she didn't think her mates had any idea of what she was up to.

It had been over a week since she had been kidnapped by Tony Picotti, and she had healed physically as well as emotionally after her horrid ordeal. Now her mates were driving her to distraction. At least one of them was by her side twenty-four hours a day, and the worst of it was they wouldn't touch her. At least not sexually. They actually touched her all the time, placing a hand to her back, arm, or shoulder, and they kissed her regularly but only chastely. She was going insane. She needed them to touch her and love her. She was sick of being treated like a fragile piece of eggshell. She was taking matters into her own hands.

She had found a moment to talk to Michelle by herself and set up some alone time. Michelle was sneaky and had told her she would get her mates' help so Talia could sneak away without her usual shadows.

Jonah had just called her bodyguard of the moment, James, for some help with something, giving Talia the opportunity to slip back into the house. After filling the tub and adding some of her favorite bath oil, she sank down into the warm water. She knew it wouldn't be long before her mates came to find her and sighed, enjoying her solitude for the moment. She couldn't wait to feel their hands and mouths all over her body as they made love to her, and if they didn't get the hint this time, Talia decided she would be the one to take control in the bedroom.

When she heard the door open, she ran her hands over her breasts and plucked at her nipples. She moaned at the pleasurable sensations running from her breasts to her cunt. She arched her neck back and slid her hands down over her belly and ran her fingers through the folds of her pussy. She heard them at the door, knew they were standing there watching her, but she didn't stop. She smiled to herself and moaned as her fingers massaged over her clit.

Talia squeaked with surprise as large, warm hands pulled her from the tub. She opened her eyes and looked into Chris's. Her pussy clenched at the heat and fire she saw staring back at her.

"You don't touch yourself, darlin'. That's our job," Chris said, his voice deeper and huskier than normal.

"Well, you haven't been doing a very good job of it lately," Talia goaded.

"Oh, baby, you are in for it now," Blayk said and began to pat her body dry with a large towel.

Her men had her on the bed moments later. To her surprise James tied her wrists together and bound her hands to the headboard. She watched them through desire-heavy eyelids as they began to strip out of their clothes. Her pussy clenched with desire when Chris, Blayk, and James stood before her gloriously naked. They each fisted their own cocks, sliding the palms of their hands up and down the lengths of their shafts.

"Please," Talia begged with a whimper.

"Please what, darlin'?" Chris asked.

"You ask so nicely," Blayk teased, "but you never say what you want."

"Please love me."

"We do love you, sugar," James replied.

"No, I mean, yes. I love you, too. Please, make love to me," Talia moaned and spread her legs wide.

Cream leaked out of her pussy as her three mates stared at her exposed, wet cunt. They groaned and closed their eyes, and she knew they were inhaling her musky scent. And then they moved as one.

James and Blayk each crawled onto the bed on either side of her, and Chris crept up between her legs. Talia squealed with relief and delight when Chris slid his hands up underneath her ass and lifted her pussy up to his mouth.

Talia mewled in the back of her throat as Chris ate her at her cunt. She moaned when she felt his warm, moist breath inside her sheath and shivered as he slid his tongue up through her folds and flicked it over her clitoris. She groaned and bucked her hips up into his mouth as he slid two fingers deep into her pussy.

"Oh God, that feels so good," Talia gasped.

"It's about to get even better, baby," Blayk said then swooped down and sucked a nipple into her mouth.

Talia's body was on fire. She couldn't get enough of their hands and mouths caressing and loving on every inch of her skin. She wanted to thread her fingers into James's hair, and she tugged her hands against her restraints. The sense of being at her mates' mercy was delicious. James kissed her and swept her tongue into his mouth. She felt perspiration break out over her body, and she keened as the pleasure of their touch sent her hurtling toward the stars. Her insides coiled tight, and she could feel liquid seeping out of her hole. Her body felt so weak as if liquid silver ran through her blood, yet so powerful as her muscles grew taut. She pulled her mouth from James and screamed as the tight spring inside her snapped and catapulted her up into the heavens. Her arms and legs trembled, as did her stomach, as wave after wave of pleasure washed over her. Chris kept flicking his tongue over her sensitive little nub and pumping his fingers, enhancing her orgasm, until the last wave slowly died. She opened her eyes and looked down the length of her body as Blayk pulled his mouth from her breast with a pop.

Talia watched as Chris moved up from between her legs and swapped places with Blayk. He lowered his head down to hers and kissed her with such love and devotion that tears filled her eyes. He lifted his head again and stared deeply into her eyes.

"I love you, Talia."

"I…I love you, too," Talia sobbed, and she reached with her arms to cling to him.

"I love you, sugar," James whispered into her ear, and then he kissed her shoulder.

"I love you, too, James."

"I love you so damn much, baby," Blayk rasped.

"I love you, too, Blayk. God, I love you all so much. What did I do to ever deserve you all?" Talia sobbed.

"Don't question it, darlin', just grab on and don't let go," Chris whispered hoarsely.

"Untie me and I will," Talia whispered back.

And grab on she did, the very moment Chris and James released her from the headboard. She reached out and took James's and then Chris's cocks into each of her hands and began to stroke up and down the lengths of their shafts. Up and down, up and down again. She made sure to give a little squeeze as her palms slid over the heads of their dicks and watched with awe as their faces grew taut with the pleasure that she was giving them. Their breathing was fast, and she could see their chests rising and falling as well as their washboard abs rippling as they thrust their hips, gliding their cocks in and out of her hands.

"Why haven't you made love to me before now?" Talia asked breathlessly.

"We were scared of hurting you, darlin'. We wanted you totally healed before we touched you again," Chris said on a groan.

"But I've been healed for over three days. You know I heal faster now that we're mated. Blayk gave me the all clear days ago," Talia whispered, confused.

"We nearly lost you, baby. We wanted to give you extra time to be well. We knew as soon as we touched you our desire would take over. We can get a little rough when we're with you. We just want to love you so damn much, we get carried away," Blayk explained.

"You're scared of hurting me? Do I look like a delicate little flower to you? I love it when you guys touch me and love me. I can't stand that you haven't been willing to make love with me. You would never, ever hurt me. Please, don't hold back on my account. I love everything you all do to me," Talia said forcefully.

"I think our little baby is need of some serious loving," Blayk said from between her thighs and moved up closer to her.

Blayk grasped the base of his cock in his large hand, and then he was pushing his way into her wet pussy. She whimpered as the delicate skin of her cunt stretched, and then his cock slid in all the way. The head of his hard rod butted against her cervix, and she thrust her hips up to him.

It didn't matter how much of themselves they gave her. She wanted more. So much more. She wanted to crawl beneath their skin and imprint herself upon them forever. She released the two cocks in her hands and reached for Blayk as he reached for her. She clung to his shoulders as he pulled her up onto his lap until she was fully impaled on his cock and straddling his thighs. She lifted her head as she grasped his hair with her hands and pulled his mouth down to hers. She kissed him with all the love and emotion she felt for him, and tasted the love he had for her. When air became necessary, she withdrew her mouth from his and stared deeply into his eyes.

Talia felt movement behind her. She moaned and closed her eyes as pleasure radiated from her ass to her pussy. Chris massaged lube into her anus, and then he pushed one, then two fingers into her back entrance. She tried to rock her hips as liquid warmth traveled to her lower extremities, but Blayk gripped her hips and held her still. The slight burning, pinching pain had her keening as Chris pumped his fingers in and out of her sheath, scissoring those digits as he stretched her tight muscles. She groaned as he withdrew them from her ass, and then she felt the large, blunt head of his cock pressing into her.

She pushed back, and he slid into her, popping through her tight ring of muscles. He held still for her, allowing her to adjust to his penetration and the packed feeling of having her body stuffed full of two cocks.

Talia groaned as Blayk and Chris began to thrust their hips, sliding and gliding their cocks in and out of her cunt and ass at the same time. She was so turned on. She could feel her juices weeping from her pussy. Her two men slowly picked up the pace, and still it wasn't enough.

"Oh my. It feels so good. Please, fuck me!" she screamed.

"We are fucking," Blayk replied breathlessly.

"More, I need more. Harder, faster, please?" Talia cried.

Something was missing. She turned her head and opened her eyes. What she needed was right in front of her face. She grasped hold of James's cock and pulled him into her mouth. She sucked him in hard, taking him to the back of her throat. She hummed and sobbed around his hard dick and began to slide her mouth up and down the length of his shaft. She pulled back and swirled her tongue over the slit of his penis, savoring the salty-sweet taste of his essence. Then she moved her mouth back over him, sucking in her cheeks to give him all the pleasure she could.

She hummed and moaned as Chris and Blayk thrust their hips into her, their balls slapping against her flesh, the sound resounding throughout the bedroom. She felt James's cock expand in her mouth, and she knew he was about to fall over the edge into orgasm. She reached for his balls, scraped her nails lightly over his delicate flesh, then pressed between his scrotum and ass. He roared as he held her head gently to him, his cock touching the back of her throat, and he spurted his cum into her mouth and throat. She cleaned him off and slid her mouth off him with a loud pop.

She was so close to her own climax, and the sensations of the friction the two dicks in her ass and pussy were nearly more than she could stand. James moved his hands, and then he squeezed both her nipples as Blayk slid his hand down between their bodies and lightly pinched her clit.

Talia threw her head back and screamed. Her body taut and trembling as her pelvic-floor muscles clamped down on the cocks in her ass and pussy. She saw stars behind her eyelids and felt her liquid release gush from her as her internal muscles contracted and released, over and over again. Chris's voice sounded in her ear as she shook between him and Blayk.

"I'm gonna come, darlin'. I'm gonna fill your ass with my seed. Are you ready?"

Chris's cock jerked, and he roared loudly as he filled her ass with his hot semen. Blayk tightened his grip on her hips, and she looked up to see his facial muscles contorting with pleasure. He pumped his hips four, five, six more times, and then he yelled and held his cock deeply embedded in her cunt as he filled her with his cum. Talia jerked and cried out as the sensations of her two mates climaxing inside her sent her over the edge one more time.

She slumped against Blayk and closed her eyes with a smile. She was cherished, content, and loved in return.

Chapter Fourteen

Talia cuddled little Stefan in her arms. The baby's tiny fist curled around her finger as his big eyes gazed up at her, and her heart melted when he smiled. She wondered if she would ever be lucky enough to hold her own child someday. She looked up to the far side of the room and saw her men were playing pool with their cousins. She often spent evenings like these with Michelle, baby Stefan, and Keira. Her days were spent gardening and her nights making love with her mates. Talia had never been so happy.

She was safe, too. Chris had told her and the rest of the pack the Feds had called to thank them for the information they had sent regarding the drug cartel and told them all the people who had worked for Picotti had been rounded up and were now currently incarcerated, and waiting to stand trial. Properties, drugs, records, and large amounts of money had been found by the FBI's computer experts. It seemed what Chris, Blayk, and James had found were only the tip of the iceberg.

At the pool table, her mates joked and roughhoused with each other. They must have felt her watching them, because as one they turned and looked at her. The heat in their eyes was enough to rev her engines, and she looked down into the sweet face of the baby in her arms.

Moments later large hands eased the baby from her and gently gave him back to his mother. James gently hauled her to her feet, and he picked her up into his arms.

"I love you, sugar," he whispered against her ear. She shivered as his warm breath caressed her ear, and she wrapped her arms around his neck as he walked toward the hall and stairs.

"I love you, too," Talia replied as she licked and nibbled along his neck.

He growled and then ran the rest of the way up the stairs to the third level and along the corridor to their suite of rooms. She had the urge to bite down on his neck where it met his shoulder, but nipped at his earlobe instead.

She laughed breathlessly as James set her down on her feet beside the bed. He held her by her hips as he stared into her eyes, and then he began to undress her. Blayk and Chris were by her side seconds later, and then she stood before them totally naked. She shivered in reaction to the heat she saw in their eyes, her pussy weeping its juices and coating her thighs. She ached so badly for their touch. She needed to feel their hands and mouths on her, loving her, but she wanted to give to them in return.

Talia took a step forward, reaching for the waistband of James's jeans. She pulled the button open, carefully slid the zipper down, and pushed his jeans over his hips. His erection stood straight up at attention, and she could see the fluid on the tip. She knelt down and licked all around the head of his cock, tasting his familiar salty essence, and then she glided her tongue down to the base of his dick. She licked along the soft, delicate skin of his sac, opened her mouth, and sucked one of his balls into her mouth. She was careful not to suck too hard because she didn't want to cause him any pain, but from the sounds of James's groans, he was enjoying what she did to him. She moved slightly and took his other testicle into her mouth. She sucked gently.

"Oh fuck yeah, sugar. That feels so good. Her mouth is so sweet," James groaned.

Talia felt another gush as her pussy creamed at James's words. Her internal walls clenched, and her clit throbbed. She released his balls and licked her way up the length of his hard shaft, and then she opened her mouth and surrounded the head of his cock. She laved the sensitive underside, hollowed out her cheeks, and slid her mouth down over him as far as she could go. She glided up over him and then back down again until he hit the back of her throat. She moaned when she felt hands around her waist and squeaked in protest when she was lifted from the floor.

Talia opened her eyes to look into Blayk's as he carried her to the bed. He was totally naked, and the sensation of his skin against hers set her on fire even more. He set her down on the middle of the bed and followed her. He covered her body but made sure to keep most of his weight off of her, and then his lips were against hers. She wrapped her arms around his neck and hugged him tight as his tongue swept into the depths of her mouth. He tasted every inch of her, and still she couldn't get enough. She dueled and swirled her tongue with his, both of them fighting for supremacy over the kiss. She moaned and surrendered her control to him when he tickled the roof of her mouth with his tongue. She was lost in sensations she never wanted to end.

Talia whimpered with frustration when Blayk weaned his mouth from hers, then he slowly pulled away from her and off to her side. She opened her eyes to see James moving to her other side and Chris climbing onto the bottom of the bed. She arched up and whimpered as Blayk and James took a breast each into their hands and began to knead them. She closed her eyes and moaned when she felt Chris slide his palms over her shins, then around to the inside of her thighs, and gently part her limbs. Talia helped by spreading her legs wide, wanting, needing to feel his touch on her sopping-wet cunt.

She sobbed with pleasure as Chris ran the tip of a finger around her dripping hole then slid that digit up between her labia. She arched her hips, begging him to touch her more. He avoided her clit at first, sliding his fingers up beside her clit and back down again. The he began to move his finger around the distended nub in circles, getting tighter and smaller until he was touching her clit.

Talia mewled with pleasure when Chris slid a finger into her depths to seek out her sweet spot. He withdrew and then thrust two fingers into her depths. Her cunt making sucking, moist sounds as his digits pumped in and out of her. The way he massaged her clit only heightened her arousal. She could feel the muscles in her womb and pussy coiling tighter, gathering in the increasing storm of rapture. She gasped and moaned when she felt Blayk and James lick over her nipples, and then the hard peaks were surrounded in moist heat. She felt Chris twist his fingers inside her, and he curled them as he pumped them in and out of her pussy.

Talia could feel her whole body trembling. Heated liquid traveled through her body, centered mainly in her belly and cunt. She felt her pelvic-floor muscles clench tight, and she froze as she hovered on the precipice of orgasm. She screamed when she felt Chris's mouth latch on to her clit, and he sucked it between his lips. The coils of tension snapped. She cried out when her cunt muscles contracted and released around Chris's fingers as he thrust them in and out of her sheath, still suckling on her clit. It was too much, but it was so good she never wanted it to end. He kept her orgasm going until stars formed in front of her eyes, and then she collapsed as the last of her climax faded away.

She gasped and moaned as Chris slowly released her clit with a slight pop and withdrew his fingers from her pussy. Her whole body felt heavy and lax after such pleasure, and she didn't know if she would be able to move again. She opened her eyes and was just in time to see Chris moving up between her splayed thighs. He had a feral glint in his eyes, and she knew he was on the brink of his control. He aimed his cock at her pussy and surged in with one powerful thrust.

Talia whimpered with pleasure as his dick separated her flesh, and she felt every ridge and pulse of his cock as he held still inside her, giving her time to adjust to his penetration. He nudged his brothers out of the way and picked her up, pulling her over his lap. His moan joined hers as his hard rod slid in another inch, until the head of his cock butted up against her womb. She looked up when Chris cupped her chin, and then his mouth covered hers. The kiss was so carnal her sheath rippled around his impaled dick, causing them to both groan with pleasure. He leaned down until her back was on the mattress once more and rolled with her on the bed, until she was lying on top of him. She pulled her mouth from his when she felt a tongue lick from the top of her ass crack down to her anus.

She nuzzled her head into Chris's neck and mewled as pleasure wrapped around her and then cried out as the tongue withdrew. Cool, wet fingers massaged over her the sensitive skin of her back hole, and then they thrust into her. She fought the natural inclination to clamp down, and she pushed back against Blayk's digits as he coated the walls of her ass with lubrication and then withdrew. She cried out again when she felt the head of Blayk's cock separating the skin of her anus. Breathing deeply and evenly, she relaxed her muscles and pushed back against him. He slid all the way into her until she could feel his balls flush with her skin. She clung to Chris's shoulders and held on as Chris and Blayk began to move in and out of her pussy and ass.

Talia turned her head when James tapped his hot, hard, silky-smooth cock against her cheek. He was lying on his side on a pillow and his crotch was practically in her face. She didn't need to be told what to do. She opened her mouth and sucked him down to the back of her throat. She followed the rhythm Blayk and Chris set up as they fucked her together and bobbed her head up and down over James's shaft.

They started off slow, speeding up incrementally until they shuttled their cocks in and out of her at a hard, rapid pace. Her heart was so full of love and joy as her men pleasured her and she pleasured them that tears of emotion leaked from the corners of her eyes. James's fingers slid through her hair, and then he gripped her gently and she knew he was about to explode. She took him to the back of her throat and swallowed. James roared as he held his cock still in her mouth and throat, and then his hot, salty cum spewed out of the end of his shaft, filling her mouth and throat with his seed. Talia licked him clean, and James pulled his now-softening cock from her mouth. He collapsed onto the bed beside her.

Talia felt the walls of her pussy give the first warning ripple of her impending climax and knew Chris had felt it, too. He slid his hands from her hips, up over her torso, and then he pinched her nipples between his thumb and finger. Molten lava flowed through her veins, and she didn't know if she could stand the heat of so much pleasure. She sobbed out loud when Chris released her nipples then cried out as Blayk's hands replaced Chris's. Chris moved a hand down between their bodies, and he gently squeezed her distended clit between his fingers and didn't let go.

Talia buried her head in Chris's shoulder and screamed as her pelvic-floor muscles gathered in and clamped down hard on the two cocks gliding in and out of her pussy and ass. She sobbed and cried, tears coursing down her cheeks as wave after wave of pleasure erupted from her womb and pussy and along her whole body. Her limbs shook uncontrollably, and her pussy gushed her liquid release.

"Look at me, darlin'," Chris panted. "I'm going to come, Talia. Watch me come."

Talia lifted her head and watched in awe as Chris's neck muscles and tendons strained as he pumped his cock into her pussy, three, four, five more times. His eyes glazed over, and the muscles in his face pulled tight. He opened his mouth and roared, holding his cock still and deep inside her, and she felt the warmth of his seed as he filled her with his essence. She had never seen such a beautiful sight, and then she couldn't see at all as Blayk thrust his hips, sliding his cock in and out of her, hard and deep. Chris squeezed her clit again, and then she fell over the edge into orgasmic rapture one more time.

She flopped down onto Chris, knowing her mates would never let her fall. She moaned when Blayk gently withdrew his cock from her ass and edged around until she could see him.

She clung to Chris as her breathing slowly returned to normal, and she snuggled against him. She had never thought to find true love with one man after her first disastrous marriage, let alone three, and here she was mated to three werewolves when she had vowed to steer clear of all men forever.

Talia had so much to look forward to, the loving and care her mates gave her, and eventually, she hoped, babies of her own. She was so happy and content, and so full of love for her men, she was bursting with it.

She eased back and looked at Chris through moisture-filled eyes. She opened her mouth to speak and then closed it again when she couldn't get the words out through a throat tight with emotion. She looked at each of her mates and knew they could see her love for them. She tried to speak again, but she clamped her mouth closed when she felt her lips tremble. Chris eased his now-flaccid cock from her body, picked her up, and carried her into the bathroom.

"We love you, too, darlin', now and forever."

Chris and Blayk got into the tub with her and washed her. She wondered where James was, but ten minutes later he walked into the bathroom and got into the shower. When they were all clean and dry, James picked her up and carried her back to the bedroom.

Talia gasped then smiled when she saw all the candles around the room, their flames flickering and waving in the air. James placed her in the center of the cleanly made bed and made sure she was comfortable leaning against the pillows on the headboard. She saw the bottle of champagne cooling in an ice bucket and four glasses beside it.

Blayk popped the cork and poured the golden, sparkling wine into glasses and handed them around. She took the glass and was about to take a sip when Chris stopped her by placing his hand on hers. She waited curiously as her mates climbed onto the bed and sat before her totally naked.

James reached behind her and beneath one of the pillows. He had something in his large hand but she couldn't quite see what it was.

"I love you, sugar. More than words can ever express," James said in a deep voice.

"I love you, baby. I was incomplete until you came into my life," Blayk said, and Talia felt her eyes fill with tears when she saw a hint of moisture in his.

"I love you so much, darlin'. You complete us more than you can know. We didn't realize how incomplete we were until you came into our lives. Will you marry us, Talia?" Chris asked, with a deep, gravelly voice full of emotion.

Talia gasped when she saw James holding a small jeweler's box open in his hand. The ring was so simple yet so beautiful. Her breath shuddered from her mouth, and tears fell from her eyes, tracking down her cheeks.

"I love you all so much. You have given me so much love, attention, and care. I would be lost without you in my lives. Yes. I will marry you all," Talia answered and launched herself into her mates' arms. They hugged and kissed her, and then they threw their heads back and howled with joy.

Her men eased her back, and Blayk plucked the white-gold ring with the one-carat solitaire diamond from the box and slid it onto her left ring finger. She stared down at the ring then back to her mates. She let them see the love she felt for her wolf mates in the smile she gave them and in her eyes, and they pulled her back into their arms.

What more could a woman ask for?

THE END

WWW.BECCAVAN-EROTICROMANCE.COM

ABOUT THE AUTHOR

My name is Becca Van. I live in Australia with my wonderful hubby of many years, as well as my two children.

I read my first romance at the age of thirteen, which I found in the school library, and haven't stopped reading them since. It is so wonderful to know that love is still alive and strong when there seems to be so much conflict in the world.

I dreamed of writing my own book one day but unfortunately, didn't follow my dream for many years. But once I started, I knew writing was what I wanted to continue doing.

I love to escape from the world and curl up with a good romance, to see how the characters unfold and conflict is dealt with. I have read many books and love all facets of the romance genre, from historical to erotic romance. I am a sucker for a happy ending.

Also by Becca Van

Ménage Everlasting: Pack Law 1: *Set Me Free*
Ménage Everlasting: Pack Law 2: *Keira's Wolf Saviors*

For all other titles, please visit
www.bookstrand.com/becca-van

Siren Publishing, Inc.
www.SirenPublishing.com

Lightning Source UK Ltd.
Milton Keynes UK
UKOW032109270513

211322UK00019B/1572/P